# SYMBOŁUM VENATORES
## COLLECTION

# WORKS BY TY'RON W. C. ROBINSON II

## BOOKS/SHORT STORIES

### *DARK TITAN UNIVERSE SAGA*

#### *MAIN SERIES*

*Dark Titan Knights*
*The Resistance Protocol Tales of the
Scattered*
*Tales of the Numinous*
*Day of Octagon*
*Crossbreed*
*Heaven's Called*

#### *Forthcoming*

*The Oranos Imperative*
*Underworld*
*Magicks and Mysticism*
*The Resistance vs. The Enforcement
Order*

#### *SPIN-OFFS*

*In A Glass of Dawn: The Casebook of
Travis Vail*
*Maveth: Bloodsport*

#### *Forthcoming*

*The Curse of The Mutant-Thing*
*Trail of Vengeance*
*War of The Thunder Gods*

#### *ONE-SHOTS*

*Maveth, The Death-Bringer*
*Mystery of The Mutant-Thing*
*Shade & Switchblade*
*Retribution of Cain*
*The Mythologists*

#### *COLLECTIONS*

*Dark Titan Omnibus: Volume 1*
*Dark Titan Omnibus: Volume 2*
*Dark Titan One-Shot Collection*

### *THE HAUNTED CITY SAGA*

*The Legendary Warslinger: The Haunted City I*
*Battle of Astolat: A Haunted City Prequel (KOBO Exclusive)*
*Redemption of the Lost: The Haunted City II*
*Consequences of the Suffering: The Haunted City III (Forthcoming)*

### *SYMBOLUM VENATORES*

*Symbolum Venatores: The Gabriel Kane Collection*
*Hod: A Symbolum Venatores Book*
*Symbolum Venatores: War of The Two Kingdoms*
*Symbolum Venatores: Mystery of the Magician (Forthcoming)*
*Symbolum Venatores: Twilight of the Gods (Forthcoming)*

## PRODIGIOUS WORLDS
*Mark Porter of Argoron (Forthcoming)*
*Raiders of Vanok (Forthcoming)*
*Praxus of Lithonia (Forthcoming)*


## OTHER BOOKS
*Lost in Shadows: A Novel*
*Lost in Shadows: Remastered*
*Accounts of The Dead Days*
*The Book of The Elect*
*The Extended Age Omnibus*
*Frightened!: The Beginning*
*EverWar Universe: Knights & Lords*
*The Horde (Forthcoming)*


## THE DARK TITAN AUDIO EXPERIENCE PODCAST
*Season 1: Introductions*
*Season 2: In a Glass of Dawn*
*Season 2.5: Accounts of The Dead Days*
*Season 3: Battle For Astolat*
*Season 4: Hallow Sword: Cursed*

# SYMBOLUM VENATORES

## COLLECTION

TY'RON W. C. ROBINSON II

# CONTENTS

# SYMBOLUM VENATORES: THE GABRIEL KANE COLLECTION



# HOD: A SYMBOLUM VENATORES STORY

# CHAPTER ONE

It is the year 930 BC as the Sovereign Solomon, King of the United Kingdom of Israel had died. Now buried with his father David and his fathers before in the City of David. Now, Rehoboam his son must take his place as he is set to travel to Shechem to be declared the new king of the United Kingdom of Israel.

Over in Egypt, under the *Twenty-Second Dynasty*, known as the Bubastite Dynasty, Jeroboam, the son of Nebat, an Israelite from the Tribe of Ephraim heard the news of Solomon's death and was relieved. Sitting in his home provided by Pharaoh Shishak, the informant also gave him a scroll detailing what's to come. He opened the scroll, beaten as it appeared and read what was written.

"His son will reign in his stead?"

"That is correct."

Jeroboam sealed the scroll and nodded.

"I will have to assemble all of Israel and speak with the new Sovereign. I hope he will not be as austere as was his father."

Jeroboam spoke with Pharaoh Shishak concerning his next motives and actions. Shishak took in Jeroboam's wishes and permitted him to achieve them, but to remember all the acts and rules he taught him while he was in hiding from Solomon. Therefore, Jeroboam gathered all he had with him and he and his wife, Ano left Egypt for Israel to meet the new king.

At the border of Israel and Phistlia, precisely around Gaza, two

Philistines were seeking to gain an entry point into the Israelite Kingdom. They saw an access point through the desert grounds.

"If we march through this valley point, we shall be able to invade and conquer without being seen. Without anyone aware."

As the two Philistines spoke, a man came out of the desert. He was alone, dressed in a brown robe and cloak. He appeared rough-looking, lean, but built physique. His face hidden from the mixture of his diadem and the sunlight. The Philistines saw him and slowly reached for their swords. Walking slowly toward the man.

"Are you lost, good man?"

"No." The man said "I am not. I am right where I should be."

"And why have you come here? To this spot?"

The man focused his gaze upon the Philistines. For his presence was of mystery toward them. They couldn't tell whether he was an Israelite or an Egyptian due to the aura around him.

"Because you're seeking to trespass."

"He's one of them!"

The Philistines rushed toward the man and was cut down within seconds by the man's skills with the sword. One of the Philistines remained alive, but mortally wounded by the blade. Backing himself up roughly through the sand and blood as the man approached him slowly. He took small steps. Slow, but steady.

"Who are you?"

"Elrad. A hunter."

Elrad raised up his sword and killed the Philistine. He wiped the blood from his beard with a cloth from the Philistine. He took their bodies and brought them across the border for all the Philistines to see, reminding them of what happens when anyone of their nation crosses the borders.

# CHAPTER TWO

In Shechem, Rehoboam arrived and all Israel greeted him with gladness and joy. For their new king had arrived. Also entering the gates of Shechem was Jeroboam and those who accompanied him. They stood out amongst the Children of Israel, yet, they themselves were Israelites besides his wife Ano. As all of Israel gathered to speak with Rehoboam concerning his ruler ship and how it will be done, Elrad entered the gates and stood in the back of the crowd facing Rehoboam. Still cloaked in his robe, he looked out and saw the joy of the Israelites and nodded quietly. Jeroboam stood forward toward Rehoboam in the eyes of the congregation.

"Sovereign Rehoboam." Jeroboam said, coming before the king. "May I speak with you?"

"What have you need to speak to me?"

"It concerns your rule. Will you rule as your father Solomon did? Will you rule over us with grievous intent? Will you put a heavy yoke around our necks as he did? Will you?"

"What would you have me do?"

"Make it lighter. Make the yoke lighter for all Israel's sake. That way, we will know for surely, you are the king Yisra'el truly needs."

Rehoboam nodded, taking in Jeroboam's words. The words were true and Rehoboam knew it. He understood the rule of his father and how it was grievous amongst the Israelites. Rehoboam turned his back to walk away and Jeroboam reached for his robe.

"Will you make it lighter?" Jeroboam asked again.

Rehoboam stood before the congregation with confidence.

"I will make a decision in three days' time. But, before I do such a great task, I must seek counsel. I believe Yahweh's will may be done.

For all of Yisra'el."

Rehoboam walked from the congregation as they began to speak amongst themselves. Voices speaking over voices. Conversations going all around the city of Shechem. Elrad watched the congregation as they spoke concerning Rehoboam and he walked away to a place for himself. Jeroboam walked into the congregation. He hoped Rehoboam would take his plea seriously and make it so. The congregation later departed.

Within the three days, Rehoboam consulted with the old men, those who were under his father's rule. For they saw what had transpired before in a generation and now they must give word to Rehoboam's rule, for the young king is uncertain of what to give the Children of Israel. Should he continue his father's way of rule or should he bring forth a lighter rule, in order for all Israel to be content. Rehoboam sat at the table before the old men, shaking his head. Unable to make a final decision.

"How do you advise me to respond to the people?" Rehoboam asked. "What should I do? Keep my father's rule or bring forth a lighter way?"

"We have a proposition for you, my king." One of the men said.

"Please, I would like to hear it."

"If you would appear to be like a servant to the congregation and serve them, then this day forth, you will answer them according to their desire. Speak good words to them and they shall be your servants forever."

Rehoboam nodded. Taking in the advice from the council.

"Is that what you believe I should do? Make myself a servant in their eyes? So, they would in turn become servants for my sake and the kingdom's?"

"That is what we advise, my king. We know no other alternative. For if you do this, the people will rejoice of your rule once more and contentment will abound by them for all of your rule and your son's rule and his son's."

Rehoboam nodded. "Thank you for your counsel. I will take it under consideration."

The old men showed obeisance toward Rehoboam as they left his sight.

Two days had passed and Rehoboam had yet to make a decision for Israel. He was torn between the advice of the old men and the request from Jeroboam. On the third day, deep in the night, Rehoboam met with some of the younger men within Shechem. For they met in one of the study rooms within the city. One preserved for the king. They came in a sat among Rehoboam, seeing the concern on his face. For he worried about the people and their response to his decision. The older men had already given him direction on what to do, but, he isn't certain of that method.

"What should I do?" Rehoboam asked. "I'm not sure what to do for Israel."

"What did the older men advise you to do?"

"They told me to become a servant amongst the people, to make the rule lighter, and they would in turn become servants to myself and the kingdom."

"I see their reasoning for such advice."

"The people said they want me to make the yoke which my father put upon the lighter. Is that what I should do? Make it lighter and become a servant to the people and they to me?"

"Well, we do have a proposition for you." One had said.

"I would love to hear it." Rehoboam said, sitting up in his chair.

"This you shall speak to the Children of Yisra'el, you shall continue your father's way of rule. When they ask of it once more, tell them your little *finger* shall be thicker than your father's loins."

The second friend entered into the conversation saying, "Now, you shall tell them whereas your father placed upon them a heavy yoke, you shall add to that yoke."

The third friend entered and said, "As your father had chastised them with whips, you shall chastise them with scorpions and straps."

Rehoboam listened carefully to those words spoken by the younger men. He nodded and a glint of a smile appeared on his face.

"Thank you for your advice. I'll consider everything before I speak amongst the congregation."

"It is what friends are for our king."

The younger men left Rehoboam's sight and after the three days had passed he stood in front of the congregation. For they all awaited an answer to their futures. Jeroboam was present for the speaking as was Elrad, who stood in the same place as before. Unlike most of Israel, Elrad was still. Calm. Collective. He neither yelled or frowned as the Israelites were doing in the presence of Rehoboam.

"He's about to speak." A young woman said to Elrad. "I hope he delivers what we asked of him."

"What he gives will be what his father commanded." Elrad said. "He's Solomon's son. He will behave as Solomon behaved to a degree. So, expect what you already know to come."

Rehoboam walked out before the people as they cheered his name, praising Yahweh for their new king. Jeroboam stood in the front of the congregation; his eyes were keen on Rehoboam. Hoping he doesn't make the same mistake his father did.

"Children of Yisra'el, you have asked of me concerning my rule for you all. And after much counsel, I have come to a decision. That decision is clear and final. For I shall not lighten the yoke around your necks."

The congregation mumbled in fear, hearing the words coming from Rehoboam. Jeroboam looked with uncertainty as a hint of anger began brewing within him. Elrad stood watch, sensing the dread coming over the Israelites.

"My father made your yoke heavy and I shall add to that yoke! My father also chastised you all with whips, but I shall chastise you all with scorpions and straps!"

"We didn't ask for this!" A man yelled from the congregation. "You're no better!"

"Oh, I am better." Rehoboam responded. "I am much better. For I am bringing forth my father's rule in greater feats and in greater strengths!"

The older men stood in the congregation, hanging their heads in shame as they knew he took the advice of the younger men, his friends over theirs. For his friends have no wisdom. No experience. They were just doing what they pleased with Rehoboam. Rehoboam left the sight of the Israelites as they echoed in anger, fear, and dread. Elrad watched as Israel was being divided before his eyes. A tragic sight for one in the twelve tribes. Yet, Elrad had remembered a prophecy spoken by Ahijah the Shilonte, stating that such an action would happen, in order to cause Jeroboam to divide the kingdom of Israel. This was all caused by Yahweh. For it was spoken by his prophet.

Elrad walked away from the shouting sprees amongst the Children of Israel. For being separate at was the only way he could obtain any sense of peace within a quickly eroding kingdom.

# CHAPTER THREE

All of Israel were grievous and stricken by Rehoboam's words and his desire of rule. Jeroboam appeared before them, giving them comfort and a hope for a brighter future. The way Jeroboam spoke to the congregation had given them a thought, that thought became an idea, and that idea became a possibility. They no longer wanted Rehoboam to be their king and to rule over them. They desired Jeroboam. For his speech and his intent towards Israel.

"What portion do we have in Dawid?" The congregation had asked Rehoboam when in his presence once more. "Neither do we have any inheritance in the son of Jesse?"

"Return to your tents." Rehoboam commanded the congregation. "See to your own tents, Yisra'el!"

The congregation did as Rehoboam commanded and returned to their tents. However, after some time had passed and the anger began to grow amongst the Israelites, they began to separate themselves from Rehoboam and his rule over the kingdom. They demanded to have a new leader to lead them into the future. Most of the Israelites had sided with Jeroboam with only the Children of Judah remaining with Rehoboam. Things were changing. Division was now seen and felt amongst all of Israel. Elrad remained where he stood, in the place of the Tribe of Benjamin.

A time later, Rehoboam remained in the city of Jerusalem and called into his study, Adoniram. Adoniram was over the tribute to Israel and to the kingdom. Adoniram was the son of Abda, a servant of Yahweh. Adoniram respected Rehoboam for his kingship and his place amongst all Israel.

"Adoniram, I send you to Shechem to collect the taxes of the people."

"My sovereign. I believe the people will not give you the taxes you speak of. For they are angry with you. Very wroth."

"Leave that to me. Go and retrieve the taxes and return. We need it done."

Adoniram bowed and left Rehoboam's sight.


For the ten northern tribes dwelled in the northern part of the kingdom, while the tribes of Benjamin and Judah remained in the southern division of the kingdom. The following day, Adoniram made way to Shechem to speak to the congregation and Elrad was there to see him leave. He knew what would happen to Adoniram and only shook his head in shame of Rehoboam's decision.


Adoniram arrived in Shechem and gathered all the Israelites in the city toward him. They knew he was one of Rehoboam's trusty men and they hesitated to hear any words that would come from his mouth. But, they hoped they would be words of change. Words of hope. A lighter hope. The people amongst him were focused. their faces stiff, but still pliable to a degree. The younger generations were only following what seemed popular, whereas the older generations hoped for what was needed.

"King Rehoboam has sent me here to collect your labor taxes and to be delivered to him this day."

"Taxes?" A man said. "Taxes?! He sends you here so we can give him our wages?!"

"It's his rule. He commands it."

"Here are our wages. We're sure Rehoboam will be pleased."

At that moment, stones began to fly toward Adoniram. Stones coming from the hands of the congregation. Smashing into his face, arms, legs, stomach, and back. He crouched down to avoid more stones. Yet, they were too much. The stones started to fall atop his head, knocking him unconscious with the following stones signaling the killing blow. Such an assault eventually killed Adoniram. In the distance, Rehoboam was present, sitting atop his horse and he witnessed the stoning. He took off, fleeing back to Jerusalem.

After the stoning, Jeroboam came before the people and spoke to them of the change and the comfort he could bring. Something in which Rehoboam will not do. Then, it was settled in the hearts of the people to make Jeroboam the king of the northern tribes of Israel. Jeroboam accepted their request and became their king. In the center of Shechem and banner was made and showcased amongst them people. For in Jerusalem, were banners of a violet menorah. In Shechem, a golden menorah shined. Signifying the divided kingdoms of Israel.

# CHAPTER FOUR

Rehoboam returned to Jerusalem and the people of Benjamin and Judah saw the fear in Rehoboam's eyes. He rode back to his dwelling place and immediately called in the elders. He spoke to them of what happened to Adoniram and the elders concluded that Rehoboam speak to the northern tribes and give them what was spoken previously. A lighter rule and a lighter yoke. Be a servant to the people and they shall become your servants. Rehoboam disapproved their recommendations and went into his chambers.

Elrad remained with his people of Benjamin and they kept to themselves. Although the children of Judah desired to speak to the king, he would not hear a word, not even more from the elders, the priests, or his friends. Rehoboam was at a loss. The following days, Rehoboam went out amongst the children of Judah and Benjamin and began rallying up the young men and older for war against the northern tribes. Rehoboam wanted revenge for Adoniram's death and a civil war was his way of receiving it.

Meanwhile, the northern tribes celebrated as Jeroboam was their king. The United Kingdom of Israel was no more. The Divided Kingdom was born. Rehoboam had gathered all the men he could. A total of eighty-thousand men. All chosen and they were already warriors. Capable of battle. They were prepared to combat the northern tribes. Rehoboam saw this as a way of not only getting his revenge, to also unify the kingdoms by force.

Near noon in the day, Elrad stood outside the gates of Jerusalem for he was led by an unseen present. It did not speak to him, only with utterance did it bring him outside the gates. Elrad looked around and only saw the grass, dirt, and trees. As he looked around, he could feel piercing eyes were upon him. Where were they is what he asked himself. Before he could turn back to the city, a black must fell from the sky and attacked him. Clawing at his robes. Elrad fought back, raising his sword and swiping the mist.
"What are you?" Elrad asked.
"You must not live!" The mist spoke. "You must not live!"
The mist swooped down against Elrad with its claws. Elrad continued using his sword to back away the strange mist and before it could reach his robes, Elrad slammed the sword into what appeared to be the mist's head and it collapsed into the grass. Elrad looked closer and knew what he was seeing.
"A djinn?" Elrad said. "Here? Why?"
The djinn was helpless as Elrad went and grabbed a vase. He commanded for the djinn to enter the vase and it obeyed. After the djinn was placed inside the vase, Elrad went out further from Jerusalem and buried it. He returned to the city after and did not speak a word to anyone concerning the djinn, only mediating on the words it spoke to him. He understood those words were indeed referring to him and him alone. As Elrad walked, a cloaked figure stood beside a tree, watching the Benjamite. He figure was hooded, wearing all black. He nodded with a smile showing underneath the hood.
"It is time." He uttered, glaring at Elrad.

# CHAPTER FIVE

While Rehoboam prepared all he had to attack the northern tribes of Israel, Shemaiah, a man of Yahweh approached him in his study. His countenance was of urgent concern and Rehoboam could see it.

"My king, I have news."

"What kind of news?" Rehoboam asked. "Is it about Jeroboam? Does it concern the northern tribes? If it does not, you may leave me be."

"It concerns them. It only concerns them."

Rehoboam nodded and sat down. He gestured his hands toward Shemaiah to come forward to the table.

"Please, tell me of this news."

"Yahweh has spoken to me. About the matters of the kingdom and what has come of it."

"What has He said?"

"He says this; thus saith Yahweh, you shall not go up nor shall you fight your brethren. Return every man to his home. For all of this is from me."

Rehoboam laid back in his chair and went into deep thought. Shemaiah stood still. Patiently awaiting a response from the king of Judah. Rehoboam considered he words of Yahweh and waved his hand.

"Very well. As Yahweh speaks, I will obey. I will tell the men to return home."

Shemaiah bowed his head and left the chambers. Rehoboam later went out and spoke to the warriors who were awaiting the notion to head out. Rehoboam told them everything Shemaiah had spoken and they knew it was from Yahweh. They gathered together and obeyed the command, returning home. While everyone was heading home, Shemaiah walked outside, seeing Elrad. He approached him keenly as Elrad turned to face him.

"Good sir." Elrad said. "What do you have need of?"

"I have no needs, son. For, I have come to deliver a message to you."

"A message? Of what sort?"

"Prepare yourself. You'll have a visitor this night and it will change the course of your life. Take heed to these words."

"My life? What do you mean?"

"You will find out when you return home. Right now, take this moment of thought and consider the costs that await you. Although, they are not many, they will become factors that charter your life in the coming age."

"I'm not understanding anything you're telling me."

"By dawn tomorrow, you will understand. You will begin to comprehend."

Elrad was left in confusion as Shemaiah took his leave.


He was not wrong when later in the night, Elrad returned home and discovered a man waiting for him. Cloaked in a rugged and torn black robe. Elrad raised his sword at the man.

"Who are you?"

He removed his hood, revealing his face. Elrad knew the face and sheathed the sword.

"I'm sorry, Prophet. I didn't know it was you."

"You have no need of apologizing, Elrad of Benjamin. You know who I am."

"I do. You're Iddo the Prophet."

"Then you do know of me."

"Many haven't seen you since Solomon's reign. Why return to the light now? Why come to my home?"

"Because prophecy speaks of you, Elrad."

"Prophecy? I do not understand. I'm just a simple man."

"Prophecy most often requires simple men."

Elrad sat down and Iddo in front. Iddo began to lay out the details to him slowly. Iddo was not seen since the death of Solomon, due to him going into self-isolation of a spiritual matter. Iddo informed Elrad he has been told to come out of the shadows to speak to Elrad about his future. His future in being part of a greater cause.

"There is an Order if you will, which exists. Many have not heard of it and many never will. They have spoken and you are one of them. One in a generation."

"What kind of Order is this? Is it like the Levities?"

"In a manner. However, the Levities aren't qualified to attest to some of the actions one must endure to become one with this Order."

"This Order, does it have a name?"

"In our tongue, it is called the *Oth Tsayad*. Elsewhere, it has many names. In times to come, a certain name."

"*Hunter's Sign*." Elrad said.

"You now see why they have chosen you to join them."

"What is their purpose? Hunt for sport and deliver the goods to the people?"

"What the Oth Tsayad do is far from the natural world. You see Elrad, the hunters target a particular kind of source. As I recall, you came into conflict with one earlier this day."

Elrad took the moment and remembered. The djinn outside the walls. The vase. The burial. All was put in commotion for this moment. All planned. All known.

"You sent that thing?"

"I did not. It appeared because things are changing. Strange entities are appearing all across Yisra'el. Ever since the kingdom was ripped in two, unusual things have occurred. Now, the Oth Tsayad has called you to stop these occurring events and place a balance within the land of Yisra'el."

"And how am I to stop these supernatural events with a basic sword?"

"I've seen others defeat far more powerful forces with a stick and a purse. I believe you can manage. You took down the djinn, which escaped from one of Solomon's temples. It was a gift from one of his wives."

"His wives are what is responsible for the time we're living in. his love for women exceeded him greatly. All into his old years."

"You speak odd of your former king?" Iddo asked. "A son of Dawid? A man after Yahweh's own heart?"

"I do not. I only speak the truth to the acts which have occurred and what are occurring. His son, Rehoboam is now seeking war with Jeroboam and the northern tribes. I desire not to fight my brethren, however, if the call comes, I will obey. For I am an Israelite from the Tribe of Benjamin. A servant of Yahweh."

"Then, you will do what I speak to you."

"What have you for me?"

"There are three trials. You must complete them and I will return to you once they're done."

"I see. Will this make Israel better for the people?"

"It will." Iddo confirmed. "In time."

"What must I do?"

"First trial requires two places of water. You must first dip yourself into the Sea of Lot ten times. This is for the northern tribes who have sided with Jeroboam. Then, you must go and travel to the Kinneret and dip yourself in its waters two times. This is for the tribes of Benjamin and Judah."

Elrad nodded.

"What must I do after that?"

"I will meet you at the shores of Kinneret and tell you there. Take a moment to pray tonight and head out in the morning. Your life changes this day."

Iddo left Elrad's home and he obeyed the words of Iddo. He prayed and took some rest. In the morning, Elrad grabbed what he needed and lastly grabbed his sword. He took a horse and left Jerusalem, beginning his trials of the Oth Tsayad.

# CHAPTER SIX

In the middle of the ongoing civil war amongst Rehoboam and Jeroboam, Elrad began his trials of the Oth Tsayad. First heading out toward the southeast to the Dead Sea. There, he stopped his horse, jumped off, and walked toward the salty water. The stench of the air was filled with the smell of salt. Its strong odor moved through the air from the gust of the wind. Elrad removed his robes and diadem, walking into the sea. He went as far as he could and dove underwater. Elrad chose to remain there for seven seconds. Afterwards, he arose and repeated the same tactic nine more times, following the words of Iddo the Prophet. Once he was complete, he dried himself off and quickly made travels up north.

Entering the area now belonging to Jeroboam and his kingdom. The Israelites of the northern tribes looked at Elrad with funny looks. They knew he was a Benjamite and believed he was confused on his goings. One older man approached Elrad on his horse. He looked concern about Elrad's doings in the northern kingdom.

"Why are you here?"

"I'm heading north. To the Kinneret."

"For what purpose?" The older man asked. "Why go there?"

"It's of urgent matter. I cannot speak of it any further."

"Our king must know you're here."

"He'll find out soon enough."

Elrad rode through the town of Adam, following the river leading toward the Sea of Galilee. He did not stop for food, drink, or rest. Elrad was focused on the cause and only death would cease his actions. Neither was his horse tired nor hungry. After the travels, he reached the Sea of Galilee and entered the water as a few fisherman looked at him strangely.

"What's he doing?" A fisherman said to another.

"Probably drunk is all. You know those types."

Elrad dipped himself two times and arose from the sea, returning to shore. The fishermen watched as he dried himself off and put his garments back on. One fisherman approached Elrad after he dressed himself.

"Good man, why go and dip in the water two times?"

"It's for the tribes of Benjamin and Judah. A sign of things to come."

"What kind of sign? A deliverance from this nonsensical war or will Yahweh return to us once again and reunite us all under one kingdom?"

"I do not have the answers you seek. Perhaps, when the time comes, you will know them."

The fisherman walked away and as Elrad turned around, Iddo was there. Elrad was startled at the prophet's sudden presence.

"How did you do that?"

"No need to know. I see you've completed the first trial."

"I did. Never expected I'll be in much water for the past two days."

"However, you've completed the trial. Good things are coming you way. Right now, I suggest you take a moment to rest. The second trial awaits you."

"What is this second trial? I should be inclined to know."

Iddo nodded and stepped forward toward Elrad.

"The second trial requires you to travel to *Har Tzion*. When you get there, a messenger will speak to you concerning the true purpose of these trials. Afterwards, you must go to *Qadesh Barne'a*, where reports have come out of a witch hiding out in the wilderness of the lands. Exterminate her and I'll be there to tell you of your third and final trial."

"And what comes after all of this? When I've done everything there is to be done?"

"You will find out. When the trials are complete."

"Get some rest, warrior. You need it for the journey ahead." Iddo turned and walked away.

Elrad went to an inn and rested for the night. Upon the brink of dawn, he arose and traveled to Mount Zion. During his travels, he continued to hear the people talk of Jeroboam's plans to face Rehoboam. The war was still going, but Elrad was focused on the trials more than the civil war. Time later, Elrad made it to the mountain and looked around. Walking across the land.

"Where's this messenger Iddo spoke of?" Elrad questioned.

Elrad turned around to see anyone. No one was near his location or in his eyesight of distance. However, when he turned and looked back, he found himself in the presence of a celestial being. Its power was strong enough to cause Elrad to fall to his knees. Elrad blocked the bright light with his shield, attempting to raise his head. He could not. He was losing much strength.

"What is this?!" Elrad yelled.

"Do not fear, Elrad. I come with no harm."

Elrad paused as the energy lowered and stood up, seeing the figure in full, dressed in linen with its loins girded with fine gold from Uphaz. Elrad knew what he was looking at and was astonished. The figure stood around Elrad's same height, but knowingly lowered it to speak to the Benjamite face-to-face. Its body was like beryl and its face appeared like lightning. The eyes were like lamps of fire. The arms and feet were like polished brass. When the figure spoke, its voice moved like a voice of a multitude. A voice of many.

"You come from the heavens. A messenger from Yahweh."

"I come from afar. Yes."

"Why? Have you come to take my life?"

"No. your time is not close. I've come for a very specific purpose."

"Does this purpose have anything to do with the Oth Tsayad?" Elrad asked. "These trials told to me by Iddo?"

"Yes. What Iddo has told you is true. You have been chosen by the Oth Tsayad to become their hunter for the land of Israel."

"Why me?"

"Because you have the qualifications of a remnant."

"So I have been told." Elrad mocked. "What have you to tell me?"

"Your future is set and your path is clear. This order of hunters. You shall bear their sign upon the sigil of the tribe of Benjamin. Every nation upon the earth requires a hunter of this order. There is no discrimination. You have been chosen for Israel's sake."

"Is this Yahweh's will?"

"You will discover that when you've completed all there is."

Elrad shook his head. He was annoyed by all he was hearing. More so by Iddo's words regarding the trials. Elrad is an obedient man and nodded.

"What must I do next?"

"Qadesh Barne'a awaits you. Help the people down there with the witch. Rid her from the land and Iddo will be there to tell you what's to come."

The messenger went away and Elrad sighed, returning to his horse for the ride down to Kadesh Barnea. Meanwhile, as Elrad went about the trials, Jeroboam was building and preparing the northern tribes for war. However, he thought to himself, in his own heart if the kingdom should return unto the house of David, then the people will go and sacrifice to Yahweh in Jerusalem and the people would side with Rehoboam, leaving him to himself. Alone and outnumbered. They would indeed kill him. Jeroboam did not want this and thought of another way to keep the people under his rule.


Jeroboam went ahead and built up Shechem in Mount Ephraim. He chose to dwell there. To live out his days in Shechem. Also, he built Penuel during these days. Jeroboam took the counsel of what to do to keep his rule remaining. The counsel he had with him commanded him of such ways and he agreed to them whatever the cost. It began later that night, the same night of Elrad's first trial, Jeroboam took gold and made two calves. He presented them to the northern tribes in Shechem for all to see. The people were confused. Some were curious. Others were happy to see something shining in their gaze.

"Is it too much for you to return to Jerusalem? Behold this day, your gods, O' Yisra'el! These are the gods which brought you up from the land of Egypt!"

The people clamored and cheered on Jeroboam for bringing these gods of gold to them. They celebrated that night as Jeroboam brought one calf and set it in the city of Bethel. He placed the other one in the city of Dan. What he had done was bring upon sin over the people as they went and began worshiping the gods of gold. His next move of ruler ship was making priests out of the lowest of the people in the region and building a house of high places.. This is a strike due to the fact the lowest of the people were not sons of Levi.


Elrad arrived in Kadesh Barnea and saw how the people moved with fear. He rode through the small area keenly. The people questioned who he was and why was he in their sight. Elrad called for the leader of the land and he appeared before him. Elrad asked about the sightings of the witch and the leader told him of the events. How the witch appeared from deep within the wilderness, striking those who traveled alone on the roads. Elrad gestured the witch didn't come for him. The leader proposed he wait for the night and head out into the wilderness, for the witch will make herself known. Elrad agreed to the proposal and rested in Kadesh Barnea for the remainder of the day.

The night had come and Elrad went straight forth into the wilderness. Sword in hand. Shield on the opposite arm. He walked out into the quietness of the forest. Only the sound of chirping could be heard and a cool whistle of the wind. As he walked further, a brushing sound acme from the trees behind him. He turned, looking up. There was nothing. The brushing continued to the point where it could be heard all around him. Elrad shrugged his shoulders, taking out a torch from his side and lighting it. The fire lit up the area and it brought out what he came for.

"Ah." Elrad said. "There you are."

The witch looked very disgruntled. Her clothing was torn as if ripped by lions or bears. Her hair was frizzy, dry, and grey as a rain cloud. her face appeared leathery and her eyes looked as if she was already dead. She stared at Elrad and saw the fire, letting out a loud screech. Elrad dropped the torch, covering his ears as the witch attacked him. Clawing against the shield. Elrad shoved her back and swiped the sword, cutting her left arm from the elbow down. She yelled and went for another attack. This time with such strength, she threw Elrad into the tree behind him.

"What was that?!" Elrad questioned.

The witch came for another attack. Clawing, yelling, and shoving Elrad across the forest. He fell backwards several times before standing up and attacking back. The witch backed up a few feet from Elrad and rushed him. Elrad took the shield and tripped the witch, then used his sword to impale her into the ground. The impact caused the witch to slow down as she struggled to stand up, but the sword was too far deep between her and the ground. The fact she was not dead caused concern for Elrad.

"Is this what I'm meant to do?" Elrad asked. "To find and kill things such as you?"

Elrad knelt down toward the witch's face, seeing her undead appearance and her cold eyes. Elrad hung his head down.

"I'm sorry this happened to you. Whomever you were."

Elrad stood up, holding the witch down with his foot as he pulled the sword from her back. He raised it up over her as she continued to struggle. It appeared whatever strength she had was gone. She was helpless.

"You've caused enough harm to the living."

Elrad slashed the sword, decapitating the witch. The fight was over and Elrad sighed with tiredness in his breath. Afterwards, he took the body of the witch and burned it. For he believed one such as her should not receive the proper burial, due to her animal-like appearance and behavior. Elrad felt there was something spiritual about her and not in a benevolent form. Sheathing his sword and setting his shield to his back, he walked away as he body burned to ash.

Over in Bethel, Jeroboam called for a feast to be held in the eighth month on the fifteenth day. The feast was similar to the one in Judah. Jeroboam brought forth an offering and gave it unto the alter. He went and done the same in Bethel. Sacrificing the calves, he made. He commanded the priests he made of the high places to go and remain in Bethel. Later in the early portion of the night, a man of Yah came to Bethel from Judah. He had a word for Jeroboam and his current actions. The man of Yah found Jeroboam standing by the alter, burning incense.

"O' altar! Altar! Thus saith Yahweh!, behold a child shall be born unto the house of Dawid, Josiah by name and upon him shall he offer the priests of the high places to burn incense upon you and men's bones shall be burnt upon you!"

The man of Yah gave a sign that same day.

"This is the sign which Yahweh has spoken! Behold, the altar shall be rent and the ashes which are upon it shall be poured out!"

Jeroboam stood and took in the words of the man of Yah. Listening closely and meditating upon them carefully. Jeroboam went to remove his hand, but he could not. He looked at his hand and saw it became one with the altar. Dried up. He pulled and wrenched. Nothing worked. His hand was part of the altar now. The man of Yah was not troubled by Jeroboam's sudden response. He was calm. Peaceful. Jeroboam turned to the man of Yah immediately, looking at him and his hand upon the altar.

"Intreat the face of Yahweh at this moment and pray for me. Pray that my hand may be restored once again."

The man of Yah listened and besought Yahweh and the king's hand was restored. He hand was as it once was. Jeroboam thanked the man of Yah.

"Come home with me, good sir." Jeroboam said, entreating the man of Yah. "You should receive some refreshment. I must reward you for the restoration of my hand."

The man of Yah responded saying, "If you will give me half of your house, I will not go with you. Neither shall I eat bread or drink water in this place."

"Why not?" Jeroboam asked. "I seek to reward you for restoring my hand."

"It was charged to me by the word of Yahweh." The man said. "He commanded me to eat no bread, drink no water, and not to turn again by the same way I came in."

"What will you do now?" Jeroboam wondered. "I desire to know."

The man of Yah nodded.

"I'm sure you do."

The man of Yah turned from Jeroboam and went another way. As he did not return the same way he came into Bethel.

# CHAPTER SEVEN

Elrad returned to his home, smelling of a distant smoke. Inside of the home, Iddo waited. Elrad set his weapons down near the entrance and went for some water at the table. Taking a moment to settle after the journey, he sat down in front of Iddo. His face was keened. He was also tired. Weary from the battle.

"You've completed the task?" Iddo asked.

"The banshee is dead. Burned to ash."

"Then, you are ready."

"As ready as I'll ever be."

"Don't be in such manner to yourself. You will need the rest for this."

"I am to fight something else? Something similar to the witch? Another djinn? Demons?"

"No. There will be no fighting in this final trial. You will be spared from that."

"What is the final trial?" Elrad wondered. "I'm curious to know."

"The final trial is very simple. Go forth and speak to the kings of Judah and Israel. Both of them."

"Speak to the kings? In the middle of a civil war?"

"It is what must be done. For all of Yisra'el and for the Oth Tsayad."

"And what shall I tell the kings? Should I give them word regarding this order hidden in the shadows? Or should I grant them advice on ending and settling this war of theirs?"

Iddo stood up from his chair and walked toward the opposite table, pouring himself a cup of water. He returned to his seat and drank. Elrad awaited word from Iddo's mouth.

"Go north and ask for a word with Jeroboam. Speak to him first. There, you will learn more than what meets the eye."

"More? What does Jeroboam know that I must know?"

"You will find out when you're in his presence."

"And what of Rehoboam?"

"Speak to him after you've had word with Jeroboam."

"Does he know something as well? Something regarding this Order?"

"Your talk with Rehoboam is about Y'israel and only Y'israel. It's past, present, and future."

Iddo finished the water and stood up from the chair, walking toward the door. He stopped and looked back at Elrad with a smile on his face. Yet, his eyes were focused on the mission.

"Get some rest and head north on the morrow. When you speak with Jeroboam, you will be astounded to what awaits all of life to come."

"I'll do my best."

Elrad rested and the following day, he traveled north, upon reaching the Shechem, Elrad is informed by word of mouth throughout the city that Jeroboam is currently placed in Penuel. Elrad comprehended the changes as to Jeroboam's different way of ruling. Elrad traveled to Penuel and there, he was confronted by soldiers. Four of them, two wielding swords and the others wielding javelins.

"Stop yourself!" A soldier yelled.

"I come to speak with King Jeroboam. It is of great urgency."

"Who sent you?"

"A man of Yah."

The soldiers took a pause and stood aside as Elrad passed through and entered the homestead of Jeroboam. Upon his entry, being led by the soldiers, Jeroboam was sitting in his study, reading a scroll. Elrad stepped foot at the door and Jeroboam's head went up with speed. He saw the figure at the door and stood from the desk.

"Who are you?"

"I am Elrad of Benjamin. I've been sent here by a man of Yah to deliver urgent words.”

“A Benjamite? Here in the north? You aren’t afraid of what the children of Judah might do or what your own Benjamites might say?”

“I care not for words or actions of the uniformed. I am here by the words of Iddo the Prophet. He told me to meet you.”

“Iddo.” Jeroboam uttered under his breath. “Ah. Iddo. The Seer.”

“You are aware then?”

“As I’ll ever be. How is he?”

“He’s well. How are you aware of him?”

“He’s the one who warned Solomon of my coming and what I was prophesized to do. Now, I look out and I see it has come to pass. But, tell me, Benjamite, why has he sent you here to speak to me and for what cause?”

“To learn of your upbringings and how you prepared for all of this. The war of the two kingdoms. Your decision to go against Rehoboam. The knowledge you gained.”

“You seek to know where my wisdom came from?”

“I do.”

“And why should I tell you my upbringing? What would someone of your stature do with the knowledge I have obtained?”

“I would use such knowledge for greater causes. Every cause that pertains to all of Y’israel and to Yahweh.”

“I see. You’re a loyal one. A loyal servant to the Most High. A true servant of all Israel. A rare breed at most.”

“Only due to this war.”

“The war is not what I wanted. I came to Rehoboam and tried to get him to see reason. To not rule as his father ruled. Yet, instead he chose to follow Solomon’s footsteps and in doing so, he has created a war. A war of two kingdoms.”

“So, do I have your permission to sit with you and learn the ways you have learned?”

“Why not.” Jeroboam turned to the soldier. “Grab this man a chair and leave us be. We’ll be here for quite some time.”

Jeroboam and Elrad sat down in the study as the king detailed everything to Elrad. From his time in Egypt and learning all he knows from Pharaoh Shishak. Elrad was taken away by what Jeroboam was describing.

"When I learned how Egypt was ruled by Shishak, he brought me into one of his briefings and it was unlike any briefing I've ever heard of or seen with my own eyes. There were no soldiers in the room. Only priests. But, these priests wore different garments than the Pharaoh. They seemed to be from other nations. Their speech was not Egyptian. They spoke of an agenda and how this agenda would cause the spiritual powers to rise from beneath the earth and aid them in battles, rulings, and in peace."

"I've never heard of something like that before." Elrad said.

"Most of the world have not heard of it period. Neither have many of the Israelites. I questioned how long this has been going. Pharaoh told me it was all happening when his father was in power and his father before. It goes far back in time. Before the Most High saved Israel out of Egypt."

Elrad listened more to Jeroboam's words of how the Pharaoh taught him the ways of a secret order. One eerily similar to the Order of Hunters. Elrad kept himself focused as Jeroboam would describe this order of worshipping a plethora of gods and all who were a part of this order were referred to as Priests. Shishak was the Egyptian priest and the others came from across many parts of the world. Jeroboam later described how he left Egypt after Solomon's death and he knew the prophecy would come to pass due to Solomon's rebellious acts against Yahweh in the form of building temples for idols in favor of his foreign wives.

"I see you were well-prepared for this." Elrad said. "For all of it."

"It is all in the will of Yahweh." Jeroboam added. "Now, I must continue with my business as usual."

Jeroboam stood up and went to the door with Elrad following.

"I thank Iddo for sending someone keen to understand my plight in this matter."

"He knows what's best."

"And where it comes from."

Elrad nodded.

"I'll leave you now, King."

"If you see Iddo, tell him I thank him for this visit."

Elrad left Penuel and made his travels back south. As he entered Shechem, he was greeted by Iddo, who was waiting for him near the entrance. Elrad stopped and stood next to the Prophet.

"Why are you out here?"

"To see if you have done what was asked and you have."

"I learned more than I was expecting to from Jeroboam."

"I see. You know where he's learned all knows. What the Pharaoh taught him."

"What of this other order? This Order of Priests?"

"Come with me."

Elrad followed Iddo to a home near the entrance to Shechem. There, the sun was slowly setting and Elrad needed the rest. Inside, Iddo and Elrad sat together as a handmaiden gave them food and water.

"The order in which Jeroboam told you is not the same as the Oth Tsayad. It is the opposite."

"Opposite in what way?"

"They are called the *Seder Kohen*. As I'm sure Jeroboam told you, they are an order of priests. All come from across the world. In joining the Seder Kohen, they all worship many gods. They also worship the spirits of the unseen."

"You're saying they do the bidding of the Adversary?"

"It is their purpose."

"And what is the Hunters'?"

"To eliminate the enemies which seek to destroy all that is good. Monsters, demons, and the like. They are enemies toward the Hunters. To the Kohen, they are all allies in this war."

"If we stop the Kohen, we can save lives."

"That is the objective of this cause. For many centuries have the Hunters fought to keep the balance in place. The Kohen are the ones who pull the cards of diversion and deceit."

"Now, shall I go and speak to Rehoboam?" Elrad asked.

"Go and speak to him. Finish your trials and all will begin."

Elrad left and traveled to Jerusalem where Rehoboam was dwelling. He arrived at the city and entered the palace. As he walked in, soldiers stared at him. Watching him like hawks. Elrad nodded to them in peace as he made his way to Rehoboam's throne room. Elrad entered and Rehoboam saw him.

"I've received word you would arrive."

"May I ask who told you?"

"A man of Yah."

Elrad nodded.

"Same with me. I guess we're here this day on familiar terms."

"So it seems." Rehoboam added. "Tell me, why are you here?"

"I've come to tell you that I am on your side in this civil war. Jeroboam seeks to do much harm to all of Y'israel and I intend on aiding you in stopping him. For your father's sake and his fathers before."

"I've heard the stories, that all of this is of my father's doing. His rebellion against the Most High has certainly shaped the kingdom and ripped it into two. Also, I hear this is what the Most High desired. Two kingdoms at war. Judah and Israel. Tell me, what should a man in my position do in such a cause orchestrated by the Creator himself?"

"I would obey to voice of Yahweh and take great heed to his word. Lead his people in the manner as your fathers before have done. To guard the commandments, statutes, and laws. To make sure your children and theirs after will have a kingdom to rule and to dwell in. not to end up as slaves to the other nations outside our borders. This is the way. This is the vision for the people. One of hope. One of honor. One of integrity. That is what I would suggest to a man in your place, my king."

Rehoboam nodded and looked over toward the elders. The elders stared at Elrad and looked at Rehoboam with a nod. Rehoboam knew the response and thanked them kindly.

"I must be grateful to have someone of your stature in both mind and spirit to be allied with the Kingdom of Judah."

"I go wherever Yahweh sends me."

Rehoboam thanked Elrad once more and the hunter left the

room. From this point forward, Elrad was mentored by Iddo concerning the ways of the Hunter's Sign. Rehoboam and Jeroboam continued in their warfare as many Israelites are being killed in battle. Elrad assisted Rehoboam when he called for him. Elrad trained himself in combat and stealth tactics. Iddo taught Elrad the wisdom of the unseen. The ways of the Hunters. After several months, Iddo presented Elrad with several scrolls. The scrolls contained information concerning monsters, spirits, and demons which have been sighted and encountered across all of Israel and outside of its borders. Elrad studied night and day aside from training and assisting Rehoboam.


Jeroboam was told by his officials of Elrad's duties under Rehoboam and he shook his head.
"I knew he was that kind of man. He's one of them. A Hunter."
"What do you mean, sir?" A soldier asked.
"It's a secret matter. I'll deal with it."

# CHAPTER EIGHT

Five years have passed since Rehoboam became king and now, the war had grown. The Kingdom of Judah had become a land of distain and deceit. Holiness was abandoned and forgotten as now the Kingdom was turned over to abominations and desolations. They built high places throughout the kingdom. Images and groves were also risen up and placed atop the highest hills of the kingdom and under every green tree that was possible. All of Judah did evil in the sight of Yahweh and in turn to their ignorance, Pharaoh Shishak was on his way to taken siege of Jerusalem.

Elsewhere in the wilderness, Elrad grew more into his calling of the Oth Tsayad. His knowledge increased as did his skill set. He spent more time in prayer and fasting. Mentored by Iddo continuously throughout the five years. Elrad would only enter Jerusalem on terms of business. He would not speak to anyone outside of his duties. He did keep to his word of assisting Rehoboam in his war against Jeroboam.

Eventually, the day had come where Shishak invaded Jerusalem with a massive arm of sixty-thousand horsemen, one-thousand two-hundred chariots, and four-hundred thousand infantrymen. The invasion came to a surprise toward Rehoboam and Elrad was present in the ongoing battle. Yet, there was hardly any fighting to be had. For Shishak took over Rehoboam's cities without a clash, leading toward Jerusalem as his final stopping point. On the field, Elrad had taken down some of the Egyptian soldiers and looked around for Rehoboam, but he was not on the battlefield. Instead, Rehoboam was crept up in his chambers, hiding from the Egyptian king.


Shishak had entered the temple, taking everything in his sight. He also took everything of value from Rehoboam's home. All of the gold and treasures were taken. Including the golden shields of Solomon. Shishak and his army left Jerusalem and the city remained standing, but it was looted of all that made it what it became. Sometime later, Rehoboam visited the looted temple and was ashamed of himself. He had the shields replaced with brass shields, a shame to himself and to the kingdom.


Elrad took the time to gaze at the temple before leaving Jerusalem. On his way out, he was confronted by Iddo, who questioned his current motives. Elrad had his horse ready.

"Where are you going?"

"Egypt. I must confront this Pharaoh."

"I know what has just transpired is a tragedy. However, this might make Rehoobam sober and turn back to Yahweh."

"That's not why I'm going."

"Then, why are you going to see this Pharaoh?"

"He's a member of this Kohen. An adversary to the Oth Tsayad. I cannot allow him to live."

Iddo nodded.

"I now see. You have more important matters to tend to."

"You comprehend them well. On the battlefield, I saw several shadows. They were not present before. They accompanied Shishak on his way here. He brought more demons to our land. Cannot let that remain."

"And when you do confront Shishak, what will you do then?"

"As any of us should. Kill him and move onward to the next."

"You truly are embracing the path."

"It is necessary. I now understand this. Perhaps, I will get more answers when I speak to this Pharaoh."

"Take care of yourself, Elrad." Iddo said. "May the Most High be with you."

Elrad nodded and rode off from Iddo and Jerusalem.


After his travels from the Kingdom of Judah toward Egypt, Elrad arrived in the city of Pi-Beseth, known in the Egyptian tongue as *Per-Bast*, a city known for its center worship of the goddess Bastet. Unknown to Elrad, a festival was taking place for Bastet. Men and women of Egyptian heritage rode on river rafts down the Nile as the men standing by played with pipes of lotus and the women on the cymbals and tambourines. Their culture was different to Israel and Elrad knew it well. It did not take the focus of the mission at hand from his mind. Several Egyptian soldiers stood guard, talking amongst themselves. Elrad leaned in closely from the nearby walls of a home, listening to their conversation.

"This is a celebration indeed." One soldier said.

"Ah. Bastet must be proud." The other soldier replied. "Did you see the Pharaoh anywhere? I was told he was here."

"He's at the temple. Has it to himself. Everyone else will be granted entry after."

Elrad received what he needed and made haste toward the Temple of Bastet. Crossing the Nile to reach the temple and as he did, he saw the cat statues of Bastet. Elrad shook himself to avoid the spiritual effects emitting from the statues. They had power and still do this day. Elrad was keenly aware. Elrad moved quietly around the temple walls, seeing only a few soldiers present, Elrad took a peek and saw Shishak, bowing own before the onyx statue of Bastet. Praising her for all she's done for him. Elrad entered the room and stood still. Shishak paused in is praise and stood up, turning around to see Elrad.

"Who are you?"

"A Hunter. Looking for his prey."

"Hunter?" Shishak noted. "Who are you and where are you from? Your speech isn't from our land. Wait, I recognize your garb. An

Israelite. Here in Egypt. In my kingdom? In a temple of our gods?!"

"I know who you are, Shishak. Who you truly are and what you have done."

"Did Rehoboam send you here as a means of revenge for what I've done? I took everything from your god's temple and he did nothing in return. Is your god truly with Rehoboam? Is he with you?"

"You will find out, member of the Kohen."

Shishak paused. Elrad stood still.

"Kohen? You called yourself a Hunter. Who are you here to hunt? Me?"

"I know of the Seder Kohen. the order responsible for many of the spiritual ramifications across these lands."

"Ah. I see. I understand now. You're one of them. Those Hunters I've heard about in my time. There hasn't been one in this lands since the reign of Khufu. There isn't one of Egypt any longer."

"I am the one within Israel."

"And you've come to kill me? To seal your allegiance to the cause of the Hunters. To rid the earth of the monsters and spirits which inhabit this and all lands?"

"I will do what I must. Jeroboam told me enough. How you taught him of the Kohen ways."

"And that is why he's succeeding in his war with Rehoboam. The Kohen properly know how to use the powers beyond for greater causes."

"It ends this day."

Shishak applauded Elrad's courageousness.

"I must ask, since you seek to eliminate the monsters and the spirits from the earth, though I am sure you've encountered your share in Israel. But, perhaps you should meet one of ours. See if you're truly capable of being a member of the Oth Tsayad as you claim to be."

Shishak chanted a peculiar spell, clapping his hands as the desert sands imploded into the temple with Shishak himself vanishing from Elrad's sight. Elrad used his diadem to cover his eyes and mouth from the rushing sands and once they receded, Elrad heard and felt the loud footsteps coming from in front of him. As he removed the diadem from his eyes, he saw himself staring in the presence of a manticore. The beast on all fours stood at the height of nine feet. It had the body of a lion with sharp talon-like claws on its feet and the face of a woman. Elrad had never encountered a beast such as this one. The manticore shrieked and stroke its paws against Elrad, slamming him into the temple walls. Elrad stood up, running on the piles of sand with his sword in hand. He swiped the beast on its legs as its spiked tail slammed down into the sand, attempting to impale him. Elrad moved over to the tail as it continued slamming and swiped his sword, cutting the tail from the beast.

"Let's see if you can conquer this one!" Shishak's voice echoed through the sands.

"Show yourself!" Elrad yelled. "Come out and face me. Don't use your monster as a cover!"

"I am among you, young one. You cannot see what truly is immortal!"

"You are but a man. Not a god."

"You do not know what you speak, Israelite. I am the Pharaoh! I am God in these lands!"

"And I have come to prove you wrong."

Elrad dodged his surroundings as the tail of the manticore continued to slam around him, digging into the sands. Erlad stopped in place and held his sword upward, he closed his eyes, keen for an attack. He stood for several seconds and the manticore lunged out from the shrouding sands, looking to attack. Elrad's eyes opened and with one sudden swipe of the sword, the manticore's throat was slashed. The beast fell into the sands and the rushing winds ceased. Elrad could see the surroundings again with Shishak staring him down from the column of the temple. The manticore shrieked in pain and Elrad approached the downed creature and raised his sword.

"Who are you supposed to be?! A hunter who only kills for his pleasures?!"

"This is who I am." Elrad said, slamming the sword upon the manticore, beheading the creature.

With the beast dead, Shishak went and grabbed his sword from the floor near the Bastet statue. He stepped forward with the sword in front. Tapping the tip of the blade to the ground. Elrad noticed him and walked toward the Pharaoh. Sword in front as well. Elrad was ready to fight. Shishak sought to eliminate the sudden threat of an Israelite in his country.

"You could abandon this sudden call of the Hunters and align yourself with the Kohen."

"Why would I choose such a life to live?"

"The Kohen are the future of this world. No matter the kingdoms which rise and fall."

"Yet, ideals live on. Hunters will always remain as long as there's prey to find and enemies to destroy."

"You see. Remnants are as but a small fracture in this world. A replete, such as myself, will always be remembered. Our work will live on for generations to come. In a thousand years, men will speak of my name and my accomplishments. Ask yourself, will they speak of you and yours?"

"What I do this day will determine that future."

"Very well, Israelite. If the manticore was not enough to kill you, then I must complete the task myself."

"You talk of rhetoric. I have heard the stories of men like yourself. High and mighty in your position. Only to be taken down by those who you set to belittle."

Elrad ran toward Shishak and the two entered a swordfight. One of brutality as neither held back their offensive attacks when made an impact. Elrad was more offense than defense. Shishak was the opposite. Shishak went to trip Elrad, yet, he jumped as the Pharaoh's foot inched closer. Elrad shoved Shishak and swiped with his sword Shishak's chest. The Pharaoh paused, looking down at his chest, seeing small drops of blood on his tunic.

"Your good. Why stop there?!"

Shishak continued the attack, becoming aggressive with each strike. Elrad deflected the attacks, elbowing Shishak in the face and shoving him back. Elrad went for another swipe, Shishak caught the attack, kicking Elrad to the ground. Shishak walked toward him in haste, sword held above his head with a sinister grin on his face.

"I thought your Israelites were tough! Get up and fight me!"

Shishak swiped the sword, Elrad dodged, rolling across the ground. He stood up and slashed Shishak's right thigh. Shishak laughed with Elrad confused to the laughter.

"Nice one."

Shishak went for another attack and Elrad deflected it smoothly. The Pharaoh went to make a step, but his leg was in severe pain that he fell to one knee. He looked up as Elrad approached him. Eyes were focused. Both of them. Elrad stood over Shishak with the Pharaoh laughing about the circumstance.

"If this is my end, do it now. Otherwise, I'll rise up and slay you here. Then, I'll return to your homeland and kill your brethren. Then, I'll take your women. Your children will forsake your ways and become adopted into the Egyptian way of life."

"You continue to talk as if you are the victor." Elrad noted. "Yet, you are down on one knee. Bleeding from the chest and leg. You are defeated, Pharaoh. You have lost."

"I have not. Neither has the Kohen. Repletes can always be replaced. My death won't change anything. All it will do is put out a signal to the others that the Hunters are out in the open once more. Then, you and your kind will wish you were dead after what the Kohen does to you all."

"Then, I shall await their visitations with my blade. You time on this earth is over, Shishak of Egypt."

Elrad impaled Shishak in his back through his chest. The Pharaoh fell dead on the temple grounds with his blood pouring out underneath him. Elrad cleaned his sword and sheathed it. He bowed is head toward the dead Pharaoh.

"May your gods be kind to you. Wherever you go."

The Pharaoh guards were heard entering the temple and Elrad made his escape as they found the body of Shishak, yelling for help as they carried his body out of the temple. In the distance near the Nile, Elrad watched, bowed his head once more and turned to walk away.

# CHAPTER NINE

Elrad made his return and told Iddo all of which transpired. Iddo congratulated Elrad on learning ore concerning the Kohen and his complete sacrifice to joining the Oth Tsayad. Elsewhere, the civil war between Judah and Israel continued on with Elrad offering his support when it was necessary. Elrad never saw Rehoboam again after several battles against Jeroboam's forces.

After some time, Rehoboam had given up the ghost and now, his son Abijam would take his place as king over the Kingdom of Judah. Word had gone out concerning the death of Rehoboam and the succession of his son. Everyone in Judah mourned the death of their king, Elrad set himself apart from the others as the days of mourning continued for thirty days.

Once the days of mourning were complete, Abijam took full reign over Judah as his mother, Maachah stood by his side. Abijam's actions were not unlike his father. He followed in his footsteps completely. Doing all he had done before and the people complained over his ruler ship. The talks of being overtly strict and his ongoing wars with Israel. Elrad knew Abijam would walk in the ways of his father, yet he knew that for David's sake, the Most High set up a son after him to establish Jerusalem as it should and shall be. In doing so of these events, Elrad took what he owned, which was not much and left Jerusalem, choosing to live in the wilderness over the sin-infested city.


Several days had passed in which Iddo visited Elrad at his small homestead out from the sights of Jerusalem. There was quietness and contentment surrounding Elrad's home. Iddo entered the home of Elrad, sitting down to eat and drink with him.

"I'm sure you're going to tell me how things are in Jerusalem?"

"As they've always been since the division." Iddo said. "Abijam continues his father's war against Jeroboam and Israel. Many of our people are dying by each other's hands. Neither side will listen to reason."

"And yet, they believe they're all hearing from Yahweh."

"That they believe. It's just, they need someone to follow. A true leader."

"Yahweh has that covered. You know he has someone already in place for when the time is appointed."

"However, such a season is yet to have come."

"And what will you do from now on till then? Give your advice to the young king?"

"I will do whatever Yahweh commands me to do."

Elrad nodded.

"But, you've done your best in aiding the Kingdom of Judah against Jeroboam's forces."

"I gave him my word that I would aid him against Jeroboam's forces." Elrad said. "Now, Rehoboam is no longer with us. My word is now in void. His son continues Rehoboam's foolish motives. I had to leave."

"That I know. But, what if Yahweh calls you back to assist Judah and protect Jerusalem from outside forces?"

"I will be there." Elrad confirmed. "No questions asked."

"Understood." Iddo said. "I have other matters to attend to in Yisra'el."

"There is something else. I did not know this Kohen was more spread out than before. It's not just Egypt they've infected, it's everywhere. Every known region to Man."

"The Repletes desire to take thrones and dominions over everyone and everything of this world. Remnants, such as yourself and those who've come before you, and those who shall come after, work in a much diverse way. You do not seek such things are carnal man does."

"How are we supposed to make change if not in the seats of authority?"

"By working in the way Yahweh works. It is mysteries to humans, yet, when you look at it further, it is not as mysterious as once before. He does his work in the midst of all. They neither see it, hear it. Nor can they smell or taste it. It is only when it has been completed that it begins to touch those in its presence. Your actions with Shishak are a primary example."

"What of the other regions out there? The nations? Yahweh does not care for them. That I stand by. But, they have demons of their own. Aren't there any who do the work for them as I am doing?"

"They have their Remnants." Iddo smiled. "Just as Yisra'el has theirs."

"Something has to be done." Elrad said. "What if I decide to head out into the nations. Clean them up of these monsters? What will come upon the world then? A better sense of peace or more terror?"

"Elrad, you cannot take it upon yourself to go out into the world and clean it up. There are others who are in those far regions doing the part of the mission."

"And I am the one in Yisra'el?"

"Precisely."

"I must ask, if there are others in every region, where was the one in Egypt? When I arrived, there was none. None to my knowledge at least."

"Not everyone gets a Hunter at the exact same time. For all you know, your actions in Egypt have already caused some major changes. Shishak is no more. Now, his son Osorkon rules in his place. Your actions have indeed brought the word of a Hunter to Egypt."

"If one does rise in Egypt, I hope to meet them. In the times ahead."

"It won't be the first of Egypt. But, only another."

"The first?" Elrad noted.

"He paved the way for many during the older days of Egypt. However, he was not one of us."

They continued to talk for several hours and Iddo left Elrad's homestead. Some time had passed, where Elrad traveled off toward south. On his travels, Elrad stopped and saw a notice stamped into a tree facing the main road. Elrad grabbed the notice and read it. The details written upon the scroll were descriptions of a strong demon causing panic in Beersheba. Whomever wrote the notice was begging for help. Help of any kind. Elrad, knowing his calling, took the scroll with him as he made his travels toward Beersheba.

# CHAPTER TEN

Elrad made his arrival in Beersheba and without a moment's notice, he was bombarded with the townspeople, begging him for help concerning the demonic presence surrounding the area.

"Please, settle down." Elrad told the crowd. "Give some space for me to walk."

While making his way into the town, a woman approached him calmly, yet with intrigue.

"You're him."

"I'm who?"

"The Hunter."

"What do you mean?"

"You have to be him. You have the appearance of a striking one."

"I've come to help with the cause."

"You saw the scroll."

"I did. I'm here to solve the problem."

"Then follow me."

Elrad followed the woman into the town. The crowd dispersed from him as they approached a home. Elrad followed the woman inside, where he saw an elderly man sitting. The man's eyes glared up toward Elrad and brightened within. The woman walked toward the man and bowed her head.

"He's here."

"You've come." The elderly man said.

"I must ask. You've heard of me?"

"You're the one who killed Egypt's Pharaoh."

"How do you know of this?"

"Word spreads." The woman answered. "The description of the killer matches your physique."

"I see. I've come to help with the town's disturbance."

"You have come to rid us of the demon."

"I read the demon was a strong one."

"Indeed, he is." The man said. "His name is Asmodeus."

"Asmodeus?" Elrad said. "I've never heard of the name."

"Asmodeus is a powerful demon. He's come to cause havoc and spread fear throughout Beersheba. There was nothing we could do but pray to Yahweh for help. By our petition, He sent you."

"I see. Where was the last sighting of this Asmodeus?"

"He was seen at one of the homes near the edge of the town."

"I'll check it out."

"Best be careful." The woman said.

"I'll be protected."

Elrad left the home of the elder and traveled to the edge of town, where he discovered the homes were attacked by Asmodeus. When Elrad questioned the owners, he realized something particular with them all. Each of them were married and the husbands were harmed in the attacks. Elrad told them to stay away from their homes come nightfall as he was prepared to face Asmodeus. Later, throughout the day before night had come, Elrad set himself apart from the townspeople of Beersheba and prayed to Yahweh until dusk had peaked in. Elrad had sought wisdom on how to deal with Asmodeus and rid him from the land. Once, the sun had set and Elrad opened his eyes, he found himself surrounded by three men, dressed in priestly garbs.

"Who are you?" Elrad asked.

"We're with the ones whom you're against. We seek what you desire to take from us."

"Us?"

"We know what you are. A Remnant of the Oth Tsayad."

Elrad's eyes keened and he grabbed his sword and fought against the three men. Killing them with quick blows to the chest and neck. The three priests had fallen. Elrad took in their words more carefully, realizing they were part of the same group as Shishak. News of the

Pharaoh's death had spread further than he realized and now he was a target of the Seder Kohen. Elrad cleaned his sword and removed the bodies from his sight.

After the fight against the priests, Elrad found himself standing in the presence of an angel. Strong in strength and might. Elrad moved back and stayed on his knees.

"Rise up, Elrad of Benjamin." The angel said.

"Who are you?" Elrad asked. "Have you been sent to help in this endeavor?"

"I am and I have. I am the archangel, Raphael and I have been sent by Elohim to assist you in your work against the demon Asmodeus."

"I praise His name. What must I do to cleanse this town of Asmodeus?"

"Head over to the waters of the river Tigris."

"Tigris?" Elrad said. "It will be daylight upon my return to this place. I sought to rid of Asmodeus this night."

"Asmodeus is not a low-level spirit. He is powerful and if you were to face him this night, he would overtake you and you would be defeated. Your duty failed and your life dust."

"I understand."

Elrad went up from his place and traveled to the river Tigris. There, he stood and a fish arose from the water, which Elrad caught with his bare hands. From there, Raphael appeared to him once more.

"Keep the fish, Elrad of Benjamin. For this is what you must do. Open the fish and remove its heart, liver, and gall."

Elrad did as the angel had said. Raphael raised his hand toward Elrad as he finished,

"Place them safely."

Elrad placed them safely in his gear and roasted the fish and ate it. Afterwards, Elrad fell asleep and arose just before dawn had set in. Raphael was there with him the entire time, watching over him. Elrad arose and asked Raphael concerning the heart, liver, and gall of the fish.

"The heart and the liver must be used to make smoke to expose the evil one. Such as evil spirits are. As for the gall, it must be used on the eyes of those who were harmed by Asmodeus' cunningness. To return sight unto them who have been wounded."

Elrad stood up, grabbed his gear and was ready to return to the site of the homes. Raphael knew Elrad's intentions and they were of a good nature. Therefore, Elrad traveled back to the homes, where the owners all came out, asking him questions concerning Asmodeus. Elrad told them he was met by an angel and the angel had prepared him for the fight against the evil spirit. As for those who were harmed by Asmodeus, Elrad used the gall to anoint them and their sight had returned to those who Asmodeus attacked. They saw the healing and praised Yahweh. This pleased Elrad and gave him more encouragement to confront Asmodeus.


While walking through the town, Raphael spoke with Elrad and told him to grab the ashes of perfume from one of the wives' living at the homes. Which Elrad obeyed. He retrieved the ashes and Raphael appeared to him, stating this very night, he would confront Asmodeus and rid him from Beersheba. Elrad was ready and prepared himself by mediating and praying.


Once dusk had come, Elrad arose and the air was silent. He went to the homes and could feel a deep eerie presence surrounding them. Elrad entered one of the homes, placing the heart and liver of the fish upon a table. Following with Raphael had instructed him to do, Elrad took the ashes and laid some of it upon the heart and lings and set a fire to it. Causing a smoke to rise up in the area of the homes. There, a loud screeching was heard from above as Elrad gazed up, seeing Asmodeus flying over the land, seeking to retreat.

"Asmodeus!" Elrad yelled. "I see you now! You cannot hide any longer!"

Elrad grabbed his bow, yet realized a natural arrow would not pierce a spirit. As he placed his bow back, a calmness set over him as he saw Raphael fly above him and snatch Asmodeus by his neck and taking him away from Beersheba. Binding him and taking him far from the land of Israel. Raphael had returned until him the following day before leaving. From that very moment, Elrad knew this would be his lot in life. To face such threats which seek to do the Israelites harm. Only with Yahweh's aid can he achieve these feats of accomplishments. Elrad now began to embrace what he has become. A member of the Oth Tsayad.

# CHAPTER ELEVEN

Sometime later after Elrad had dealt with Asmodeus, King Abijam had gathered the Kingdom of Judah together and went to Mount Zemaraim to face Jeroboam and the Kingdom if Israel. Abijam tried to gather all of Israel together, proclaiming Yahweh is their true leader. However, Jeroboam did not take heed to the words of Abijam and went to war with the son of Rehoboam. Abijam was well-aware of Jeroboam's attack and the armies went into battle with one another.

In the distance near the mountain, Elrad sat upon his horse and saw the battle commencing. Elrad no longer placed himself in political matters that were outside of his hand or purpose. Elrad shook his head in shame and gazed up to the heavens.

"How long will our people kill one another? How much bloodshed is needed to repent for past sins?"

When Elrad was looking in the sky, he caught a glimpse of something above him and the mountain. He keened his eyes, seeing the hovering figure. It appeared to be wheels within wheels, turning at a quick speed. Elrad saw eyes upon the wheels and they were looking down toward the battle. Elrad jumped off his horse, watching the object in the sky.

"In the Holy One's name, what are you?" Elrad wondered.

The object continued turning and bolted high in the sky above the clouds. Streaking like a lightning bolt. Elrad looked and saw it was gone.

"You were watching it all." Elrad uttered under his breath. "You know what's to come."

# CHAPTER TWELVE

Elrad traveled to Jerusalem after the months had passed from the Battle of Mount Zemaraim. Upon arriving in the city, Elrad went into the caverns of the Well of Souls. There, Elrad stood alone and went down on both knees and prayed. He continued to meditate on all he learned from Iddo. He mediated on the ongoing war between the two kingdoms and what was to come of Israel's future. Elrad raised up his head, seeing the stone structure sitting before him.

"I now make this proclamation. I am Elrad. Born of the Tribe of Benjamin. Circumcised the eighth day. Taught in the ways of my forefathers. Instructed the ways of the Torah. Raised by a father who feared Yahweh. Nurtured by a mother who feared Yahweh. Now, I stand as a man. A man on my own. After what I have seen and heard from the divided kingdoms and the revelation of such secret groups, I now make this known before heaven and earth. I will protect all of Israel from the principalities and rulers of darkness in this world. This is my heritage and will be until the breath has gone from my body. I am no longer referred to as Elrad of Benjamin by my brethren for I am a Remnant. I am now Elrad, a Hunter of the Oth Tsayad.

THE BATTLE OF ZEPHATH

# CHAPTER ONE

In the year of 911 BC, Elrad the Hunter made his way into the city of Jerusalem. Still under the rule of the Kingdom of Judah, which began with Rehoboam after the death of Solomon. Ever since, there has been war between the Divided Kingdoms of Israel. The city is still reeling from the effects of the civil wars. Now, Elrad stood before the current king of Judah, Asa.

"You are Elrad aren't you?"

"I am."

"From what I've heard from my father and his father before, you are a loyal servant to this kingdom. To Judah."

"I am loyal to Yahweh first and foremost." Elrad answered. "My brethren come after."

"I am aware. However, I have summoned you on an urgent matter. The Kushites and Egyptians have assembled themselves together to face us. It is only a matter of time before we face them in battle. I would like you to stand with us against them."

"Against the Kushites and Egyptians? I have had my rounds with them before. Primarily Egyptians."

"Will you stand with us?"

"It is only Judah whom they seek to attack? What of the other Kingdom?"

"This matter does not concern them. This is of Judah and only Judah."

Elrad nodded.

"Very well. Since I am from the Tribe of Benjamin. Judah is where I stand. I will stand with you in this battle."

Asa nodded with a smile.

"Then it is settled. When the time comes, I will call for you."

"And I will hear your call just as I hear the words of the Living Yah."

# CHAPTER TWO

Elrad left Jerusalem and rode off to Kadesh-Barnea, where he was greeted by Oded the Prophet in a midst of a crowd. Some saw Elrad on the horse and turned away for fear of being targeted. Words of Elrad's past actions have spread throughout both kingdoms of Israel and Judah. Elrad went off his horse and approached the prophet, showing him much respect.

"You received my message."

"I did." Elrad said. "You said you wished to speak to me about something important. I would like to know what it is."

"Follow me."

Elrad followed Oded into one of the homes. Inside, they sat down and ate. After a brief moment, Elrad turned to Oded, asking him the purpose of this meeting. Oded sighed and nodded.

"You are aware of the Kushites and Egyptians? And what they intend to do?"

"Asa told me."

"Did he mentioned the leader of the Kushites?"

"No. who is the leader?"

"He's called Zerah."

"From the way you're telling me this, I assume this Zerah isn't just a general to the Kushites."

"Because Zerah is one of the Repletes. One of the Kohen."

Elrad was now more inclined to hear the words from Oded. He leaned in closer with intent.

"How are you certain?"

"Zerah came to know of the Kohen from Shishak. I know you remember what happened to him."

"Of course."

"Now, Zerah looks to bring the Kohen into Judah through the means of this invasion. Being an ally to the Egyptians, he rallied an army of both Kushites and Egyptians. Now, he plans on invading Jerusalem and taking the city in a siege."

"This is what Asa is aware of." Elrad replied. "But, he does not know what Zerah's true intentions are?"

"He does not."

"Then, I must alert him."

"Before you return to Jerusalem, you must make travel to the Dead Sea."

"The Dead Sea? Why?"

"Because there's a small coup of Egyptians looking to sneak their way in. I know you're a man of silent tactics. If you can stop them before they make a closer move, you will give Asa an advantage in this battle."

Elrad nodded.

"I'll head that way and see what needs to be done. Thank you, Prophet."

"Take care, Remnant."

Elrad left Kadesh-Barnea and made his way toward the Dead Sea.

# CHAPTER THREE

Elrad arrived out to the Dead Sea, seeing the southern portion surrounded by a small army of Egyptians. They were armed and relaxed. Elrad stepped off his horse and hid in the nearby bushes facing the waters. Elrad noticed the sun was dimming and decided on striking in the darkness of the night. After several hours passed, the Egyptians became drunk with their beer and just as fast as a lightning bolt, Elrad attacked them and killed them. He left the area soon after as their bodies were discovered by another arsenal of Egyptians the following day. Word had spread of the small army's demise just as Elrad was riding down to road to Jerusalem.

In Jerusalem, Oded had met with Asa to discuss the possibilities for a incoming battle against the Kushites and Egyptians. Oded had told the king of his talks with Elrad and Asa was pleased. He was ecstatic to know the prophet had spoken to Elrad, due to Elrad's previous allegiance in the early civil wars with Israel and Jeroboam.

"There is one thing I must ask, prophet." Asa said.

"Tell me."

"Does Yahweh stand by our side in this battle? Is it his will for us to face the Kushites and Egyptians in war?"

"Well, for starters, you have turned Judah around to obeying Yahweh and his commandments. You were granted rest and you restored and built much in this kingdom for the tribes which reside. Yahweh is with you and when it comes to facing your enemies such as these Kushites and Egyptians, Yahweh is on your side."

"Thank you, prophet. I just wanted to be sure."

"You're not doubting are you?"

"I am not. I only wanted clarification to the cause. That way, we can be certain Yahweh's will prevails in this endeavor."

From the doors of the chamber, Elrad entered. Showing obeisance to Oded and Asa.

"How did it go?" Oded asked.

"The Egyptians are dead." Elrad answered. "It was only a small army of them. Twelve at most."

"This gives us an advantage." Asa said. "Yah be blessed."

"Indeed." Elrad replied.

# CHAPTER FOUR

It was on this day in Jerusalem, where Asa rallied his soldiers of Judah to travel out to the Valley of Zephath to face Zerah and his armies. Judah had five hundred and eighty thousand warriors strong. Elrad arrived as they were exiting Jerusalem to the point where Oded had approached Elrad with caution, for Elrad was ready for the battle ahead.

"You must heed this word, Elrad."

"What word?"

"When you are out there to see the battle take place, remember to gaze to the sky. For Yahweh has something in store for the enemies of His people."

"You mean He will aid us in this war physically?"

"I am not certain. But, He will aid you and you shall prevail. Only remember, your duty in this battle is to confront Zerah and put and end to him before more of the Kohen's doctrine spreads throughout all of Judea ."

"I will. Thank you, Prophet."

Elrad jumped upon his horse and rode off with the armies of Judah toward Zephath.


Elsewhere, Zerah was doing the same with a mixed multitude army of Kushites and Egyptians. Their faces were stern, yet determined. With Zerah's guidance, they had absolute faith and belief they are prepared to win this battle. Their numbers even outweighed all of Judah's army combined with one million warriors alongside three-hundred chariots.

"This battle is ours." Zerah said to himself. "For the Kohen."

58

# CHAPTER FIVE

Asa and all of Judah's soldiers came out near Mareshah, to the Valley of Zephath. Elrad was present with them, keening his eyes on the surroundings. From above and below. A watchman looked ahead before them and pointed.

"They're here!" He yelled.

On the other end was Zerah with his soldiers. Their combined army gave the appearance of a large mass. Asa saw that he was outnumbered heavily. The men of Judah began to tremble at the sight of Zerah's army. Zerah chuckled and clapped his hands.

"Is that all you have brought?!" Zerah yelled. "Did Yisra'el not come together at such a dire moment?!"

"This battle is ours!" Asa screamed.

The armies of Judah moved forward into the valley. Elrad had followed them from the side, monitoring Zerah's movements only. Zerah waved his hand as his army went forward and the battle begun. The men of Judah eliminating the Kushites and Egyptians, however, Zerah's army begun to prove too different as they had the numbers. Elrad jumped into the battle, slashing his way toward Zerah.

Elrad moved through them like a speeding arrow, which caught the attention of Zerah. He leaned in toward his right-hand man, pointing.

"Who is that man?"

"From what I've learned, he's one of those Hunters. From the *Oth Tsayad*."

"A Hunter of the Tsayad." Zerah said. "Here in this battle?"

"My Lord, I believe he's here for you."

Zerah turned to his right-hand man and grinned. He grabbed his sword, jumping from his horse.

"Then I must ask him."

Zerah ran into the battle, slashing those who he saw in his path. He savored the moment while Elrad pursued him with vigor. Just as they were inching closer, more of the soldiers of Judah clashed with the Kushites and Egyptians, causing a enclosure between the two. Elrad looked out as Zerah pointed toward him with his sword.

"Another time, Hunter!"

"No." Elrad said to himself.

Elrad followed Zerah, while Asa looked around the battlefield. Seeing the sight of killing, the scent of blood in the air mixed with the sand on the wind. Asa quieted himself and exhaled.

"I know what I must do."

Asa stepped forward and went down on his knees, looking up toward the heavens.

"Elohim! It is nothing with You to help, whether with many or with those whom have no power, help us! O' Yah our Elohim, for we rest on You! And in Your name, we go against this multitude. O' Yah, You are our God, let no man prevail against us this day!"

From Asa's last words, Elrad caught a sense of something around the battlefield and without haste, the Kushites and Egyptians began to fall dead on the ground in the sight of all who were present, including Zerah. The Egyptians were killed as were the Kushites. Some of the remaining Kushites ran and fled the scene, Asa saw them and rallied the men of Judah to chase them down. Zerah knew he was defeated and fled the area with Elrad following.

Asa and the men of Judah pursued the fleeing Kushites all the way to Gerar and the Kushtites were quickly overthrown by Asa and the men of Judah. Afterwards, they killed the cattle which belonged to the Kushites, carried away the sheep and camels. All in abundance. They spoiled and some all the cities around Gerar before returning to Jerusalem. While they were preparing to leave, Asa looked around for Elrad.

"Where is Elrad?"

"He went after Zerah." A soldier answered.

"Then, justice will be done." Asa nodded.

Zerah continued running until he was out of breath. He stopped himself in the midst of another valley, not one in similar size to Zephath. He sighed and turned around to see Elrad standing behind him, sword in hand.

"You know why I've followed you."

"I do. You're one of them. A Hunter of the Tsayad."

"Then, you know the purpose of this meeting."

"I do. If you should know, Shishak was the one who taught me the ways of the Seder Kohen. I saw you fleeing the area after you murdered him in the temple."

"As you have said, prepare to visit your mentor in the afterlife."

"I would fight you, but, as you can see, I'm out of breath. Give me a moment to catch myself in full."

"No."

Ah, very well. For the Kohen!"

Zerah swiped his sword toward Elrad's face, which Elrad blocked with his own sword. He two clashed swords while maintaining their stances and distance from one another. Zerah tossed dirt into Elrad's eyes and went for a blow, yet Elrad caught his movements and slashed Zerah's arm from his body. The sword fell to the ground as Zerah went down on his knees.

"Give me a good death at least."

"I will give you what you deserve." Elrad said. "All who belong to the Kohen will feel the same end as you."

Elrad impaled Zerah in his back and walked away from the scene as lions descended on Zerah's corpse, dragging it away into the bushes. Elrad continued walking back to his horse and once he was upon the horse, he caught the glimpse of an object in the sky above the Valley of Zephath. He recognized it clearly.

"You again."

What Elrad had saw was the flaming wheel within a wheel as it disappeared into the sky. Elrad nodded. Riding back to Jerusalem.

# CHAPTER SIX

All of Judah celebrated their victory in Jerusalem. Asa and all of Judah praised Yahweh for their victory and for the spoils of war. The following days after, peace was brought upon them and was made between Judah and Egypt after news had spread of the battle's outcome.

Elrad, stayed to himself in a room, studying the flaming wheel he's seen. He questioned their purpose and desired to know more. Now, Elrad had another task upon himself, to find out what they truly are and what must he do to find the answers he sorely desires.

*"Where will You take me next, O' Yah? What do You desire of me in these hours of my life? I seek Your wisdom. More than ever."*

# WRATH OF THE ANAKIM

## CHAPTER ONE

Elrad was in the city of Jerusalem, reading through many of the scrolls in the temple. He searched thoroughly for any details pertaining to the fiery wheels he saw in the sky. While Elrad searched, he was greeted by Oded.

"Elrad."

"Prophet." Elrad nodded.

"I must speak with you."

"Where?"

"Here is fine." Oded replied, sitting down next to Elrad.

"What have you come to tell me?"

"A member of the Kohen has been sighted."

"Here in Jerusalem?"

"No. In Ashdod."

"Ashdod? Why would we concern ourselves with those outside our sphere?"

"Because this member of the Kohen to my knowledge is gathering an army to invade Judah. That we cannot allow."

"You're saying you want me to go into Ashdod and confront this Kohen member?"

"Yes. you're the only one of the Oth Tsayad here in Judah. It is your duty to make sure the Kohen do not make a return into our land."

Elrad nodded. "I will do my best to find out who this member may be."

"It won't be easy. As word tells of the member being associated with the Children of Anakim."

"Anakim? I thought this would be just a simple task."

"When you arrive in Ashdod, look for a man named Joel, he will give you more details than I know. He's seen the member of the Kohen and his whereabouts. He knows all."

"Very well, I'll get going as soon as possible."

# CHAPTER TWO

After a day of travel, Elrad arrived in the city of Ashdod, seeing himself surrounded by the Ashdodites. He shook himself and continued walking into the city. While, watching his surroundings, a young man sped up toward him, dressed in a dark grey tunic. His hair was slicked back and his beard was in the early stages of growth. Elrad paused himself with his hand slowly next to his sword.

"You aren't from around here are you." The young man said.

"How can you tell?"

The young man gazed at Elrad's all black robes with the violet sash. He clicked his tongue and pointed.

"By the way you're dressed. Ashdodites don't wear the same apparel as you do."

"Nice touch. Good day."

"Wait a second, stranger. I am Nibhaz and I will be your guide on this journey of yours."

"Thanks, but I do not need a guide. I'll find my own way around."

"Then, how will you discover the member of the Kohen?"

Elrad paused, turning back toward Nibhaz.

"What do you know of the Kohen?"

"A lot. I'm the one who told your prophet about their workings here, Hunter."

"You gave Oded the details."

"Yes. And now you have arrived to cleanse our land of the Kohen."

"You have the wrong idea. I've come to stop them from invading Judah. Nothing more."

"But you are here in Anakim territory. You are eliminating the

Kohen from out land is just as righteous as protecting yours."

"What do Ashdodites know of righteousness?"

"You would be surprised."

"If you know so much about the Kohen and the Hunters, why haven't you discovered who the member might be? Take them out for yourself?"

"Because my task is to observe and to inform. Not to fight."

"I see." Elrad replied. "Tell me what you know."

"Not here. Follow me."

Elrad followed Nibhaz to a secluded area. One in which Nibhaz thought was quiet enough. It was a tavern. Of a kind. Elrad followed Nibhaz into the tavern alongside the keen eyes of the Ashdodites staring him down. Elrad didn't make a move toward their gestures as he kept his focus on the cause. Nibhaz found a table and sat.

"Tell me what you know." Elrad said.

"Here's what I know." Nibhaz said, grabbing a bottle of wine from the nearby table, taking a drink.

"Keep going."

"I heard of some operations being done over in Gath."

"Gath? I thought the details were here?"

"Things travel and move through these parts. I'm just an observer."

"I see. And what of Gath?"

"There are two brothers in Gath. They keep close tabs on all the workings of the Kohen in these lands. They are the ones who have the answers you seek."

"And these brothers, I'm assuming they're Anakim?"

"Yes. They surely are. Remember Goliath of Gath? These two are from the same bloodlines. Distant cousins I was once told by a priest."

"Good of you." Elrad stood up. "Now, I will head out to Gath and confront these brothers. See what they know of the Kohen."

"Um. One small thing." Nibhaz gestured.

"And that is?"

"The brothers won't give you the answers willingly. They're a bloodthirsty bunch. They kill for sport and they abhor foreigners.

Especially Israelites."

Elrad chuckled.

"Makes things easier for me."

"I'll be seeing you around?" Nibhaz said.

"Only if you're still alive." Elrad replied.

"Good enough."

Elrad stood up from the table and left the bar. Heading out to travel to Gath.

# CHAPTER THREE

Elrad had arrived in Gath. He shook his head when he arrived. "First Ashdodites, now Gittites."

Elrad walked through the city as the Gittites were staring him down. Elrad paused himself, standing still. He nodded his head as some of the men were approaching him. Swords in hand. Elrad reached to his sides, raising up his sword and grabbing his shield from his back.

"I have no quarrel with any of you."

"You're trespassing on Philistine land, Israelite!"

"I have come to speak with the Brothers of Gath. Tell me where they are and I will soon be out of your lands."

"You will be turning back and leaving."

"I am giving you all one last chance. Back away and tell me where the Brothers are?"

"Israelite thinks he can command us to do his biddings. We don't serve you."

"Very well." Elrad sighed. "This is all on you."

The Gittite went for a strike and Elrad dodged the attack and swiped his sword, cutting off the man's arm with the sword in hand. He screamed in pain as the other surrounding men went to attack Elrad. Elrad fought them off with sword against sword. Others went for punches and kicks, yet, Elrad was able to maneuver their moves with ease.

"How are you moving like this?" One asked with fear.

"I have my ways."

Elrad killed another man as the rest fled. Elrad turned and

continued walking through Gath, until he heard several large footsteps approaching. Elrad nodded to himself before turning around to see two tall figures. Each one standing well over seven-feet tall. Their bodies were broad. Fiery red hair, piercing brown eyes, each carrying large weapons, dwarfing Elrad's own.

"Who is this?!" One said.

"He's not one of us. Look at his garb."

"He must be from the further north I would say."

"Why not south?"

"Because, it's obvious this man's an Israelite."

"An Israelite. Here in Gath. In our city."

"I am." Elrad replied. "You two must be the Brothers I've been told about."

"Heh, and why would an Israelite have such interest in the Brothers of Gath?"

"Because I am not just an Israelite. I am something else. I hear you have some keen knowledge into a certain order. You're aware of someone within it and I have come to meet them."

"You won't get such answers out of us so easily."

"Figured I wouldn't. which is why I ask the both of you, tell me where this Replete is and I will be on my way."

"No. We don't give up our brethren."

"I guess they'll find out when news spreads of your deaths."

The Brothers burst out in laughter. Shaking their heads and fanning toward Elrad.

"It's two of us, boy. Only one of you."

"Haven't you heard the tale of King Dawid? Remember how he killed one of your own in his youth. What of the Battle of Gob? Where a man named Elhanan slewed Goliath's brother? You've heard the stories."

"We don't fear no Israelites."

"I'm not the one you should fear. Remember, Dawid slung the stone, yet the power of Yahweh was behind it. Elhanan did battle Goliath's brother, yet Yahweh was with him. My Elohim was with them both and I proclaim this day, He is with me."

The Brothers took their guard. Gripping their weapons tightly.

Elrad's eyes were focused. His hand holding his sword. Only silence moved through the air between them. One of the Brothers blinked and roared. Rushing toward Elrad and within seconds, Elrad swiped the Brother in the throat with his sword and the giant's body fell into the dirt. Elrad paused himself before facing the second Brother.

"You… you killed him!"

"He went first." Elrad said. "Now, will you comply with my offer or suffer the same fate as your brother?"

The giant looked at his spear and Elrad. Breathing heavily. Elrad didn't move. That notion caused the Brother to scream with anger as he went to impale Elrad with the spear. Elrad dodged and slammed the sword into the spear, cracking the wood. Elrad stomped the spear into the ground before running toward the giant and jumping in the air, stabbing the giant in his eye with the sword. The giant fell in the dirt just as his brother with Elrad standing over him.

"Didn't get what I came for." Elrad said to himself.

Echoes of applause sound off behind Elrad, grabbing his focus quickly. He turned to only see one man. A man dressed in royal garb. He had his sword on his side as he applauded, looking down at the bodies of the Brothers. He nodded, giving a gesture of respect to Elrad.

"I see you've taken out the Brothers of Gath. A rather extraordinary accomplishment."

"Who are you?"

"I am King Achish. Now, who are you and why have you caused such a distress in my city?"

"I am Elrad. A Hunter."

"A hunter? What kind of hunter are you?"

"Not your typical one."

Achish nodded and paused. His eyes caught it. A smirk grew on his face.

"I see the insignia on your sash. You're one of them. A Benjamite and a Hunter? I get it now."

"I asked the Brothers to give me the information I came for. They refuse and now, here we are."

"You seek the Replete."

"You know him?"

"I do. However, he is not here in Gath."

"Then, where is he?"

"In Gaza. On business."

"His name?" Elrad asked.

"Head to Gaza and ask for the man named Anak. He's the leader of the Anakim. Now, I'm sure he won't be too hard to find."

"Leader of the Anakim? You speak of the giants."

"Yes. However, they are much larger and fierce some than the Brothers you slew so easily. Plus, the animals in their lands. Stronger than a barbary lion."

"I see. But, if you know about Anak and his allegiance to the Kohen, then what are you to them?"

"One who sees what's to come in the future for us all. A chance to bring a much greater order to all nations. Not just the ones we're aware of."

"By seeking justice?"

"Not in full."

Elrad nodded and walked toward his horse. Once he was atop, he saw Achish staring him down.

"I will add," Elrad said. "If we do cross paths at another time in similar circumstances, I will put you down as well. If the Tsayad give the order."

"And I you, if the Kohen does the same."

Elrad turned away and rode out of Gath.

# CHAPTER FOUR

Elrad rode into Gaza and once his horse had stopped, he found himself staring at a dozen men. All of them were in the heights of Goliath and the Brothers of Gath. Walking through them was another man, dressed in armor with long red hair. He stood before the dozen men and faced Elrad.

"Who are you, stranger?"

"I've come to meet with the member of the Kohen." Elrad replied. "I know he's here."

"The Kohen. Ah, your insignia. I know what you are."

"Then you can tell me where the Replete is."

"Replete. That's who you're looking for?"

"That's why I'm here."

The man chuckled as did the other dozen men. Elrad raised up his sword and impaled it into the ground, gaining their attention.

"Where is the Replete?!"

"You're looking at him, Hunter." The man said. "I am Anak, leader of the Anakim. All whom are left."

"Then, you know what's about to happen."

"Really? Is this what you want? To go into combat against me. Someone who is much taller and larger than you are?"

"You are my target."

"Why fight when I can explain everything about the Koehn to you. Perhaps, it can change your mind. Alter your spirit and convince you to convert to our ways."

"Not possible. I have made my choice."

"A choice is always reversible. But, you can make a new one.

Forsake the way of the Hunters, forsake your Israelite heritage, and forsake your god. Join us and you will be forever remembered for all generations to aspire to."

"Foolish gains. Fight me."

"No. instead, you will face something else."

The ground started quaking and jumping up from behind the men and Anak was a four-legged beast. Snarling as it lunged toward Elrad. Elrad dodged the incoming attack and found himself staring at a huge beast. Its hide resembling the desert grounds, covered with a large dark mane and golden piercing eyes. The beast was even bigger than the men and Anak.

"What are you?" Elrad said.

"This creature is what we call, the Beast of Anakim. Let's see if you can kill this magnificent animal and perhaps you are truly who you claim yourself to be."

# CHAPTER FIVE

Elrad dodged away from the quickening swipe from the Beast of Anakim. He ran further out into the fields as the animal followed. Anak stood back with his men and grinned. Clapping his hands together. The Beast roared toward Elrad, who took in a deep breath. Holding his sword and shield tightly with a firm grip.

"Your move." Elrad said.

The Beast lunged once more with Elrad spinning himself around the creature and slashing its hind leg. Elrad paused himself as the Beast turned. Anak was keen on the battle. Elrad ran toward the animal sword over shield and swipe the side of the Beast before being tackled by the animal's right paw to the ground. The Beast jumped over Elrad, trying to bite for his head, Elrad raised his shield to block the jaws of the Beast. Struggling his best for strength.

"You are done, Hunter." Anak yelled. "Give up. Convert to our ways and forsake your own. Only then, will you be able to survive this day from the teeth of our creature!"

"I will not forsake my walk. This fight is mine."

Elrad reached over with his left hand toward his sword, clutching the sand with his fingers as the weight of the Beast began to increase. Elrad grunted, stretching his arm toward the sword. The Beast swiped at the shield, slightly bringing it down. Elrad raised it again just as the Beast' teeth impacted. Elrad looked over to the sword, touching it with his fingers and sliding it over as best he could. Anak took a step forward.

"What is that man doing?"

Elrad pushed the sword closer to his palm and grabbed it tightly. The Beast stood back, going in for another lung. The Beast jumped and Elrad raised the sword. The Beast fell over Elrad, leaving the area silent. Anak smiled, yet was unsure as to what happened. The animal was not moving. All Anak and his men could see is the animal's back, seeing it's laying on its side. From the other end, Elrad arose, sword and shield on hand. He exhaled as he looked out toward Anak and his men.

"That's not possible!" Anak screamed. "How could he kill one of our beasts?!"

"You seem to forget an important part in all of this, Anak!" Elrad yelled. "I have a better god than you do."

Anak snarled. Foaming from his mouth. He commanded hsii men to charge and kill Elrad. However, his men did not move, causing a disturbance in his leadership. Anak turned forward to his men, screaming at them to go out in the field and kill Elrad. They did not obey his command. While yelling at them, Elrad was making his way toward them. With each step Elrad took forward, Anak's men took steps back. Before Anak could figure out what was happening, Elrad plunged the sword through Anak's back and his men fled the field. Anak fell to the ground and Elrad stood over him.

"My duty here is done." Elrad said. "Another member of the Kohen eliminated."

"You will… never understand… our ways." Anak spoke slowly. "We will never be truly gone from this… world. Never."

Anak took his last breath and Elrad turned around and left Gaza.


Days later, Achish was resting in Gath as news came through of Anak's death. Achish took a small moment to mourn a fellow member of the Kohen and from there, two peculiar figures approached Achish in his home. They were dressed in all white robes, wearing golden crowns over their heads. Achish saw hem and bowed.

"My Lieges."

One of the men handed Achish a scroll, which he opened and read to himself. After reading, he closed the scroll and looked up toward the two men and only grinned.

# CHAPTER SIX

Elrad returned to Jerusalem and spoke with Oded about what happened in Ashdod, Gath, and Gaza. Oded nodded and congratulated Elrad on completing the task at hand. Elrad returned to his home to rest. The following days after, Elrad went back to his studies of the flaming wheels. He took a moment of rest and walked outside. He gazed up to the sky for a only a quick glance and from there, something caught his eyes.

"Can it be?" Elrad said to himself.

The object vanished from his sights just as he saw it. A ball of light, nearly bright as the sun streaking across the sky with its trail quickly disappearing from sight. He sighed and returned inside. Later in the weeks after, Elrad was given orders by Oded of another Kohen member roaming around the borders of Judah. Elrad agreed to the task, grabbed his sword and shield, and rode out of Jerusalem on another mission. Oded now knows completely that Elrad is indeed a Hunter of the *Oth Tsayad* and his works have only just begun.

# THE RISE OF THE MUMMY'S TOMB

## 1863
# EGYPT EYALET

It is the beginning of summer as the Monster Hunter and Ufologist, Gabriel Kane travels to Cairo, Egypt by ship to investigate the Pyramids of Giza and the ancient tombs of the old leaders. He also seeks on discovering if extraterrestrials had any part in the construction of the pyramids and had any influence on the pharaohs of old. Even though it is at risk from the ruling Ottoman Empire.

Upon arriving in Cairo, Kane, wearing a brown hat and trench coat, he searches for a camel to use in order to gain access toward the location of the pyramids. He ends up finding a man who is selling camels and he approaches him.

"Camel will cost you." The Camel seller said.

"I know. How much for the camel?"

"I personally accept gold or silver."

Kane smiled as he pulled out five shekels of gold and three shekels of silver from his coat pocket. The facial expression of the Camel Seller changed in an instant, showing excitement and shock.

"That will do, my good sir. That will do."

The Camel Seller accepted the shekels of gold and silver from Kane and gave him the camel. Kane mounted onto the camel and set his sights toward the pyramids that were in his eyesight within a distance.

"Move it." Kane said to the camel.

The camel began to move as Kane kept his eyes of the pyramids.

Kane continued his movement toward the pyramids as night

immediately approached and covered him along with the landscape. Kane decides to stop and allow the camel and himself some rest before arriving at the pyramids, which are within a three to six-mile radius of his location.

Waking up along with the sunrise, Kane mounted back onto the camel and moved along closer to the pyramids. Kane raises his head upon entering El Giza, seeing the Great Sphinx in the horizon as he approaches the Pyramids of Giza themselves. Astonishing in some form by their height and size, he began to wonder how the structures were built and how much strength was needed to complete a task of that size.

Kane mounts off the camel and begins his investigation on searching and studying each of the three pyramids. He begins with the smallest one, known as the Pyramid of Menkaure. Already with the knowledge of the pyramids as tombs for the pharaohs, Kane searched the smallest one for any details concerning extraterrestrials either involved with the building or with the pharaohs themselves.

"I understand and know of the legend of Herodotus." Kane said. "Believing how Menkaure was more of a benevolent Pharaoh than the ones that came before. So, it may be."

Kane entered the mortuary temple of the pyramid and discovered how the foundations of the inside were made of limestone. Kane glanced down at the floor and realized they were made from granite and had granite facing surrounding him by way of the walls.

"Judging by the minerals it took to build this thing, this must have taken a long time to complete and this is just the interior."

Kane looked and seen what appeared to be an inscription in the temple. Kane stared at it while deciphering the language. After deciphering, Kane understood the inscription stated that the temple was made as a monument for the Pharaoh's father, who was the king of upper and lower Egypt. While inside, Kane also discovered carved images of the old kingdom and understood it due to its high presence of evident details it held.

Kane continued his search of the Menkaure pyramid, before deciding that he should search the other two before the next nightfall. Kane continued his search with only a little water to drink and hardly ate anything before his investigation of the pyramids. Kane finished his search of the Menkaure pyramid. He set his sight on the second pyramid, known as the Pyramid of Khafre or Pyramid of Chephren. The second tallest of the three pyramids. Khafre is the tomb of the fourth dynasty pharaoh Khafre, who had ruled from the time of 2558 till 2532 BC.

The Khafre pyramid has the length of two hundred and fifteen point five meters leading to seven hundred and six feet. The rising height of the pyramid went from one hundred and thirty-four point four meters, equaling four hundred and forty-eight feet in height.

"Amazing are these structures."

Kane had understood that the pyramid may have been robbed ages ago and decided to head straight toward the burial chamber of the pyramid. Kane had questioned if the pyramid possessed two locations of entry, but he never figured it out to be exact. He continued walking until he had entered the subsidiary chamber. Which had opened from the west of the lower passage. Kane believes the chamber was used to store precious items that belonged to the pharaoh or anyone close to him. The passage above appeared to be made in a clad of granite, which descended into a horizontal passage that lead Kane straight toward the burial chamber. Kane followed the passage directly.

Kane found himself standing inside the burial chamber. Kane looked at the size of the chamber and noticed it was carved from the bedrock through a pit. The roof of the chamber was constructed of limestone beams that appeared to have been gabled. Kane saw how the chamber had a rectangular shape and stared at the sarcophagus of Khafre. Seeing how his coffin was carved out of complete block of solid granite and how it had sunk into the floor. Kane looked down closer to the sarcophagus and seen what appeared to be small animal bones laying close to the coffin.

"Animal bones. Hmm."

Kane looked around and decided to leave the Khafre pyramid and to finally search the third pyramid, the largest of the three and the most known one of the three pyramids. Kane exited the Khafre pyramid as he stared at the Great Pyramid of Giza, also known as the Pyramid of Khufu or the Pyramid of Cheops. The Great Pyramid is the oldest of the pyramids in the Necropolis Giza area.

Kane searched the three known chambers of the pyramid. Going through the three of them in the amount of time he had left until sundown. The lowest chamber appeared to be cut from bedrock and laid where the pyramid was built, however left unfinished. The second and third chamber were the King's and Queen's chamber. Kane noticed that the pyramid was the only one to possess ascending and descending passages. The three smaller pyramids near the Pyramid of Khufu appeared to have belonged to his wives.

While searching, a loud bang had sounded from the outside, gaining Kane's attention, he rushed out of the pyramid to the outside to see what caused the loud noise. Kane had exited the pyramid and found himself standing in the presence of an ancient Egyptian army with a living mummy in front of them.

"What is this?" Kane said.

Kane continued to stare at the Egyptian army and the living mummy that apparently led them. Kane slowly reached for his pistols on his side until the mummy took a step forward in front of him.

"Who are you and how are you even alive?" Kane said.

The mummy spoke in Egyptian and Kane could understand the ancient language the mummy had spoken. Kane gripped his pistols tightly, waiting for the mummy to strike with his army.

"You are Akhenaten." Kane said. "If that is the case, then why are you over here?"

"I am here to tell you to leave this land before the curse falls upon you and those that will follow you in the future."

"What curse will follow me into the future?"

"It appears as if you lack spirit and do not seek to understand the curses that dwell in this land. The curses that those before you in times past felt, the plagues that ran their course on this land and the curses of the ancestors that lived here in times past."

"You won't be able to fool me, Akhenaten. The curses will not affect me in any way because I know what is going on around here."

"Be that as it may, stranger. But I warn you to leave this land at once."

"So, I take it that this curse of a mummy's tomb is your doing. You're the mummy that folks say has risen several times and placed curses on those who entered this land in search of knowledge."

"I warn you to leave. This is your final warning, stranger."

"I won't leave." Kane said as he fired his pistols toward Akhenaten and his army.

Akhenaten didn't make a flinch as the bullet flew past him without any harm. Kane continued to fire before placing the pistols back in their holsters as he pulled out his sword and ran toward Akhenaten. Akhenaten placed his left hand in front of Kane, shoving him back a few feet as lights shined down from the sky. Kane partially covered his eyes to see where the lights were coming from and seen three unidentified flying objects in disk shapes, hovering over the three pyramids of Giza.

"What is this?" Kane said. "The flying disks."

The sun had set, and the moonlight shined down upon the area. Kane looked above the disk and noticed the pyramids were in the exact alignment with Orion's belt in space.

"Interesting placement they did."

Kane turned to see Akhenaten, but he and his army had vanished without any noise being sounded. Kane turned back to the three flying disks as they began to levitate higher in the air and leave at warp speed. The sky was clear of the disks and silence filled the area. Kane nodded with his hat and turned away, seeing his camel still sitting in the same location as he left it. Kane makes the decision to leave the area as his theory had presented itself before him in the form of Akhenaten and the three flying disks.

# THE UFO CRASH OF 1863

# NOVEMBER 28 1863
# AMERICAN CIVIL WAR

During the night, something mysterious in the sky is falling towards the ground. As it falls, it glows a reddish-green color and coming down faster and faster. It slams into the ground and is stuck there. The next day, Confederate soldiers discover the crash and take the object to one of their bases. Their leader, Robert E. Lee confirms that it was only a bombing accident but didn't tell them the description of the object. He commands his soldiers to take the object in their possession and to keep it highly secret.

On a ship, heading towards the United States, is Gabriel Kane. A monster hunter and ufologist. Kane is a man in his early twenties. Twenty-Three exactly. He's lean and gloomy, somewhat somber-looking at times for his age. His skin appears pale with his cold eyes. His face is shadowed by his hat. He is dressed entirely in black and is equipped with a weaponry that features a rapier, a dagger, a cutlass, a saber, and a pair of flintlock pistols.

He arrives in the United States to discover the crash site. As he travels across the northern lands, he runs into a group of confederate soldiers, who are weary of his presence.

"Identify yourself, sir." One soldier said.

"I am Gabriel Kane. Monster hunter and ufologist from Europe." Kane said. "I am here to visit the area of which an object crashed."

"There was no crashed object." The soldier said. "I believe you've been given wrong information. Now, return to your home."

"I don't live here." Kane said. "I came across the Ethiopic Ocean on ship. I heard directly that something fell from the sky around this area. So, that's why I'm here and my information is never wrong."

"This time it is." Another soldier said. "Now, leave this area at once, boy."

"Just tell me where the location is." Kane said.

One of the soldiers smacked Kane in the face with the butt of his rifle. Kane's head turned quickly before he wipes the blood off his mouth and turns to the soldiers, smirking.

"If that's how you want to play it." Kane said.

Kane kicked the soldier and knocked him to the ground. He looked toward the other two soldiers standing by, who ran toward him, Kane fired at them with his flintlock pistols.

Kane defeated the soldiers and continued looking for the crash site. As he continues searching the woods, he sees tracks on the ground in front of him. Kane walks over to the site and kneels, tracking the snow around the area. He looked up and spots something buried in the snow. He walks over and wipes the snow from it. It's a metallic object, a small, but heavy piece. Kane picks the object up and examines it. With his confused expression he says that this object appears not to be man-made. He puts the object in a small bag and continues walking toward the nearest town, just a few miles north.

Kane sees the town in front of him, surrounded with a few wooden buildings. He enters the town and sees the Union soldiers. Kane walks up to one of the soldiers and get his attention.

"Excuse me, but do you have any idea about the crashed object?" Kane asked.

"I'm sorry, sir. Who exactly are you?" The soldier asked.

"I am Gabriel Kane. I am a visitor from Europe."

"From Europe." The soldier said. "Why would you be in a place like this, especially during these times."

"I don't understand what you're talking about." Kane said.

"As of right now, we're in a civil war. North versus South." The soldier said. "See, me and the others you see around here are Union soldiers, the north. While the men in red are the Confederate, the south."

Another soldier in the distance calls out to the soldier speaking with Kane. He looks and tells Kane that he should look out for himself and that he might have to choose a side if he decides to stay a little longer. Kane looks on as the soldiers leave the town, heading into the forest. Kane walks through the town, looking at the buildings and certain areas. He sees both soldiers and civilians throughout the town. He decides to buy a map of the area and he looks through it. Going through the forest and heading to Adams County. Kane leaves the town and heads back into the forest, following the map.

Kane arrives west of the woods and discovers a frontier, surrounded and occupied by Confederate soldiers. Kane smiles at the sight of them, as if they're just targets to be taken down. Kane hides in the bushes to avoid any contact with the soldiers. He looks to his right and sees a group of them carrying an object of a large size, the object is covered with a blanket of sorts. The soldiers take the object into the large building in the middle of the frontier. Kane decides to sneak into the frontier, passing by soldiers swiftly. As he moves faster, he runs into a soldier.

"Who are you?" The soldier said.

The soldier took Kane's hat off and slammed it. Kane raised up and looked at the soldier. From behind Kane, more soldiers appear and eventually surround him. Kane notices that the soldiers are seriously hiding something due to their level of secrecy of hiding in the forest. The soldiers grab Kane and take him to the head center of the frontier. Inside the center building, sits Jefferson Davis. Davis sees the soldiers bringing in Kane.

"What are you doing?" Davis asked.

"We found him sneaking into the frontier, sir." The soldier said. "We caught him just in time."

The soldiers hold Kane in the center, facing Davis. Kane looks at Davis.

"What is your name?" Davis asked.

"My name is Gabriel Kane." Kane said. "I'm only here to investigate the crash that occurred in the woods."

"There was no crash." Davis said. "It was only an accident that happened out there. What could possibly crash?"

"There had to be a crash." Kane said. "I saw tracks and I found debris."

Davis stared deeply toward Kane. Staring him in his eyes with a slight confusion in his face."

"Debris? Of what?"

The soldiers let Kane go as he reached into his pocket, showing Davis the metallic piece that he found. Davis' face expression changes drastically, showing a sign of nervousness, along with an expression of anger.

"I found this piece in the woods, right around the crash site." Kane said. "The object was here in this spot."

"Ah! This doesn't prove anything!" Davis yelled. "Take him away."

The soldiers grabbed Kane by his coat and dragged him out. Once they reached the outside, Kane head butted the soldier and kicked the other one in the gut. Kane ran off into the forest as the soldiers began firing at him. Kane entered the forest and the soldiers run after him. Kane continues to run deeper into the forest as the soldiers track him by his footprints in the snow. As the soldiers follow the tracks, Kane turned left of the forest, his footprints disappear since there's little snow in the area. Kane continues moving and the soldiers lose tracks of the footprints.

"He couldn't have gone far." One soldier said.

The soldiers turn back and return to the frontier. Kane has now entered a complete grassy area, with only little snow. The sun shined down on him, as his hat have given him shade. As Kane continues walking, he looks at his map for the surrounding areas.

"Where am I?" Kane said, looking at the map. "What is this location?"

He looks at the grassy locations, not seeing nor hearing a single sign of life anywhere close. As he continues to walk forward, he spots a group of soldiers, wearing blue uniforms on horsebacks. Some are walking behind them. Kane stops and stands still as the leader of the Union soldiers comes toward him on his horse.

"Who are you, sir?" Kane asked.

"I am Abraham Lincoln." he said. "The President of The United States."

Kane is taken along with Abraham Lincoln and a group of Union soldiers to their frontier. Upon arriving at the frontier, Kane looked around the location, scouting the area for any sign of Confederate soldiers. Lincoln signaled to Kane to follow him inside the frontier. Kane followed him into the frontier.

While entering the frontier, Lincoln sat at a table and waved his arm toward the other seat which faced him. Kane looked and wondered.

"Please sit." Lincoln said. "We can talk right here."

Kane sat down at the table, facing Lincoln. Other Union soldiers walked in and out of the frontier. Many of them stayed outside guarding the location. Lincoln signaled the nearby soldiers in the frontier to stand guard outside, leaving him and Kane alone inside to discuss what's taken place. The soldiers exited the frontier leaving Kane and Lincoln inside at the table. Lincoln offered Kane some water and he took the cup. Both drank the water before speaking to each other.

"If I may ask, Mr. Kane. What were you doing out there?"

"I was running from some Confederate soldiers, sir. They were chasing me until I ran into you and your soldiers."

"When we found you out there, we didn't see any Confederate colors wandering about. So, why were they chasing you if I may ask?"

"I'm a resident from Europe. I came over here to investigate a crashed object that fell near this location. When I was searching for the object, the Confederate soldiers took me in and claimed that no object crashed, but I found evidence that goes against their words."

"Where is this evidence that you speak of? Do you possess it on you at this very moment?"

"I do."

Kane reached into his coat pocket and pulled out the metallic-like object. He handed over to Lincoln, who looked at it and rubbed his chin, questioning himself about the object. He handed back over to Kane, who placed it back into his pocket.

"I've never seen a texture like that in my lifetime. You believe the crashed object was made of that material?"

"Yes sir. I found this little fragment at the crash site. I didn't find the whole object. Someone took it and has hidden it from the eyes of many."

"I take it you believe the Confederate took the object and has hidden it from the people and mainly the Union. Might they believe the object could give them some form of extra help in this war that's taking place?"

"Whatever the case may be, sir. The object is not something to be toyed with. It possesses power of unspeakable energy. Energy that this world has yet to study and figure out."

Lincoln nodded while lying back in the chair. He took another sip of water from his cup and looked over at the door, seeing the soldiers walking about and keeping guard. He raised himself up from the chair closer to the table. He lies his arms across the table.

"I figure that you align with us and we can find this object you're speaking of. That way we will know for sure if the Confederates have taken it and are planning to use it for their own personal gain against us and the North. What do you say to that, Mr. Kane?"

Kane sat quietly, thinking to himself. He looked toward Lincoln and extended his hand. Lincoln extended his and both shook on the agreement.

"So, where do we head toward to find this object?" Lincoln said.

"We'll have to enter their domains. The only way to be sure about the whole situation."

"It's a fair start."


At a Confederate frontier, Jefferson Davis speaks with other Confederate soldiers about Kane's whereabouts. He questioned them on where he could have run off to and if he was a spy sent by the Union and Lincoln. The soldiers declined the statement and said he was only a man looking for the object. Davis walked out of the frontier and looked around the location. Giving himself some air from the inside.

"For goodness sake. We must find that man. By any cost."

Kane stood outside the frontier along with Abraham Lincoln discussing way of entering the Confederate frontiers. Lincoln gathered some soldiers to accompany them on their investigation. Gathering the soldiers, Lincoln considered the possible cost of having his men die because of a alien craft being hidden.

"I truly hope there's a craft." Lincoln said.

"There is a craft and you'll see it for yourself when we get to the destination."

"I believe your word, Mr. Kane."

Kane and Lincoln gather their supplies and head out for the Confederate base where the spacecraft is hidden. The Union soldiers follow them with their rifles in hand.

Upon leaving the base early on, Davis and a group of Confederate soldiers find a Union army base and immediately attack. Davis yells out orders to destroy anything and anyone they find within the base. The Confederate soldiers ransacked the base, destroying all that sits in the base. After the search, no Union soldiers are found by Davis and his Confederates.

"You cannot tell me that we've been made fools of." Davis said. "Where are they? Where could Lincoln be?"

Traveling a few miles from their base, Kane and Lincoln see a Confederate base in front. Kane sights no sign of Confederate soldiers nearby. He points out toward the base as Lincoln looks ahead.

"I see no bodies around the area." Kane said. "Shall we enter in?"

"Be cautious I warn." Lincoln said. "We don't know if this is a trap played by Davis and the Confederates."

They approach the Confederate base slowly, hiding behind the snow-covered trees and bushes to avoid possible sight. Kane looks around and sees no one, the area is as quiet to the point where only bird could be heard or the falling snow from the trees.

"This place is abandoned." Kane said. "We have our opportunity here, Mr. Lincoln."

"Where would they keep this craft, you speak of?"

Kane sees a large settlement ahead that sits near the back of the base. He points toward it.

"That's where it would be."

Kane mounts off the horse and runs toward the large settlement as Lincoln follows him and commands the Union soldiers to keep watch of the area in case Confederates appear to enter. Kane reaches the settlement and enters it and Lincoln looks around at the base before entering the settlement himself. Once they both entered, their eyes were locked on the craft, which sat on the ground in the middle of the settlement.

"This is it." Kane said. "This is the craft that fell from the sky."

"You were speaking the truth, Mr. Kane." Lincoln said. "Now I can see you're a man of your word and a loyal one."

"Don't give too much credit ahead of the victory."

Kane walks over to the craft and examines the encryptions and designs that are carved on the craft's surface and understands that it is an alien spacecraft. He pulls out his notes from his coat pocket and compares the drawings to the carved images on the craft. He sees that they are one in the same.

"This is an alien spacecraft indeed." Kane said. "There's more to the universe than what we know."

Kane and Lincoln immediately hear shots fired from the outside. They rush to see what's taking place and discover the Union soldiers firing at the Confederates that have appeared to the base. Lincoln looks ahead toward the entrance of the base and sees Davis with them.

"Men, we must leave at once!" Lincoln said. "We'll take this battle out into an open field!"

"You're planning on ending this now." Kane said.

"You don't have to stay with us any longer, Mr. Kane. You'll already found what you've been looking for and now you can continue on with your journey into the mysterious."

"No. You helped me and now I must aid you in your war against Davis and the Confederates."

Lincoln nods.

"Let's leave now!" Lincoln said.

The Union soldiers begin to leave the Confederate base. Davis shoves soldiers aside and sees Kane with Lincoln. He points toward them with anger in his eyes.

"There's that adventurer! He's traveling alongside Lincoln! I knew he was a Union soldier to begin with!"

The Union soldiers leave the base. Davis moves quickly to see where they're heading, and he spots an open field in front of them. He looks to his Confederate soldiers and hands them more rifles.

"We head toward that open field and we eliminate these Union soldiers for good and we take down Lincoln and this adventurer!"

The Confederate soldiers cheer as Davis leads them toward the open field. Kane looks back and sees Davis and the Confederates coming behind them near the field. He gets Lincoln's attention and points. Lincoln looks back and sees Davis coming. He smiles.

"Let them come and let them die."

Kane stands with Lincoln and the Union soldiers in the snow-covered field awaiting Davis and his Confederate soldiers to appear before them. The Union soldiers are ready for combat just as Kane and Lincoln are. In front they see Davis approaching and the Confederates at his back. Lincoln points out at Davis.

"This is the moment where this civil war will end." Lincoln said. "No more bloodshed upon this land amongst Americans battling Americans."

"Let's go ahead and finish this, Mr. Lincoln." Kane said.

The Union soldiers are ready as Davis and the Confederates face them. Both the Union and Confederate are opposing each other in the open field as it snows down above them. Davis smirks at Lincoln and Kane.

"I see you have the adventurer at your side, Abraham."

"I do and he is keen to do his work and move on from this."

"This is not his war. Its ours. The North versus The South. Nothing More. Union or Confederate and he made his decision to become a Union fool."

"We didn't want this war between us, yet you've asked for it and now you have it. For right here, it ends for good and there's no reason to continue this bloodshed on this land amongst Americans."

"Enough of your words, Lincoln. Let's get to the bloodshed."

"Suit yourself, Jefferson Davis of the Confederate."

The Confederate soldiers quickly run toward the Union, which do the same as Lincoln and Davis stand behind and watch the two armies run to each other in battle. Kane stares at Davis and glances at the armies battling it out amongst each other.

Shots are being fired and some are stabbed to death with blades. Davis looks at Kane and points at him. Kane spots Davis pointing and decides to approach him. Lincoln stops Kane as he walks toward Davis.

"What is it?" Kane said.

"Do not kill Davis. He's lost within his mind."

Davis looks ahead at Kane and Lincoln and laughs.

"Why are you holding the man back, Abraham? Afraid that he'll fail before you and give the Union a bad name on your expense?"

Lincoln looks at Kane. Concerned, yet trustworthy.

"Be careful."

Kane begins to approach Davis until the sky lights up above them and the battling armies. Kane looks up, holding his arm up to avoid the blinding light from above. What Kane sees is an alien spacecraft above the battlefield. Lincoln and Davis also spot the craft above them. Both are afraid, fear settling in their hearts at the sight of the large object.

"Oh my." Davis said. "It is real."

"What is it doing, Kane?" Lincoln said. "Why is it just sitting above us?"

"I do not know."

The craft begins to charge up as the sound of its engine begins to roar. Kane decides to get away from the battlefield. He pulls Lincoln alongside him.

"What are you doing, Kane?!"

"We have to get away from this area immediately! The craft is about to shoot down at us!"

Davis continues to stare at the craft, seeing its energy forming from beneath it. He is astonished at what he sees.

"Oh, how you can aid us in this war. The possibilities are endless."

The craft shoots down a beam of energy on the battlefield, separating the remaining Union and Confederate soldiers. Kane and Lincoln are behind a set of trees to avoid the blast. Davis is knocked to the ground at the impact of the beam. Kane looks up and sees the craft take off into the sky and it vanishes. The area is now quiet with a large burnt circle in the battlefield with melted and burned snow.

A few days later, Lincoln announces the civil war is still ongoing and the Union soldiers are preparing for more battles against Davis and the

Confederates. Kane has taken the crashed craft with him on a ship as he returns to Europe to study the craft even more so than he could within the woods of a civil war going country.

# THE UNDEAD AND THE EXTRATERRESTRIALS

## 1866
# FEUDAL JAPAN

Three years after The UFO Crash of 1863, Monster Hunter and Ufologist, Gabriel Kane has now taken a trip to Japan to study of the ancient Japanese history and its culture. Now, during the final years of Feudal Japan. Kane is highly aware of its history and looks to discover more about it.


Kane, now twenty-six, three years after his involvement with the American Civil War, has learned a lot more about his occupation as a monster hunter and ufologist. Kane, wearing what appears to be a grayish-white trench coat and hat, with red Japanese markings on the coat, arrives at a small museum in downtown Edo. Inside the museum are dozens of artifacts containing amounts of history about Japan and the early years of Feudal Japan. Kane looks at one book and reads about its history.

"A very interesting history here." Kane said as he looked through the book.

Kane continues to look through the book and the museums, loud screams are heard from the outside of the museum. Kane, quickly turns and runs outside. Once outside, Kane sees a swarm of zombies. The zombies appear to be wearing ancient Japanese armor and gear. The zombies turn to Kane and run after him. Kane pulls out a sword and runs through the zombies, slicing them apart. As he slices through them, they spew out a liquid which is glowing green. One of the last zombies runs toward Kane, Kane moves toward the right and slices the head off the zombie's body.

After fighting off the zombies that surrounded the area, Kane kneels and examines the green liquid. As he gathers some in a small container for experimentation. Once, he stands up the Shogun military arrive. They stare at Kane, knowing that he's a foreigner. They walk over to him, speaking in Japanese.

"You are to come with us, sir." One soldier said.

"Very well." Kane said. "If you suggest it."

Kane holds his hands out as the soldiers handcuff him and take him onto their carriage back to their base.

Once they arrive at their base, they bring Kane, who's blindfolded, into a sort of interrogation room. They sit him down in a wooden chair and leave the room. Kane listens to see if anyone is inside the room. Hearing no sounds, he finds a way to take off the blindfold and looks around at the room. The room is completely covered with Japanese art from each wall. The room resembles a samurai dojo room to an extent. Kane looks behind him and sees the brown wooden double doors.

"Would like to speak with someone, please." Kane said, speaking in Japanese. "Anybody around here who I can speak with?"

Kane hears the double doors open, a Japanese man, wearing a white robe walks into the room with two Shogun soldiers. They stand on both sides of Kane as he looks in front of him, seeing the Japanese man.

"Do you really believe your staring will frighten me?" Kane said to the man. "I've come across worse."

The Japanese man stands silently while staring at Kane.

"For starters, where am I?" Kane said.

The Japanese man walks closer to Kane. Kane looks up at the man, seeing hardly any emotion in the man's face.

"You, sir, are in Edo Castle.' The man said.

Kane pauses as he begins to think. He looks at the man, startled.

"If we're in the Edo Castle, that makes you the Shogun." Kane said. "You're the military dictator of Japan."

"I am Shogun Yoshinobu." The man said, "The seventh son of Tokugawa Nariaki, daimyo of Mito."

"So, you're the current Shogun." Kane said. "But you said you'll never step foot in this castle nor Edo if you were Shogun. Why are you here?"

"I had to break my vow because of your troubles." Yoshinobu said. "For that reason, you must pay gravely and by gravely, I mean dreadfully."

Kane tries to break free of the ropes tied to his hands. Yoshinobu walks around him, quietly.

"You destroyed our test drill and that is why you must pay with your life.' Yoshinobu said. 'You've come into my country and disturb my governance.'

Kane continues to sit in the chair with his hands tied together behind his back as Shogun Yoshinobu walks around him in circles and later sits in front of Kane. Yoshinobu stares in the eyes of Kane, who does the exact same.

"Why don't you just kill me while I'm here." Kane said. "Because you know, I'll be out of here immediately within seconds."

"Your courage doesn't frighten me." Yoshinobu said. "Though my creations will certainly frighten you."

"Don't even bother trying to have your inventions to frighten me." Kane said. "Like I said, I've seen much worse."

Yoshinobu stood up.

"We know who you are, boy." Yoshinobu said. "You're Gabriel Kane, that monster hunter, ufologist man."

Kane stares at Yoshinobu.

"How would you have known?" Kane said.

"We've heard about your tale of being abducted by higher beings." Yoshinobu said. "We even heard about your tale in the Americas."

"So, I'm sure you know how that ended." Kane said.

"It doesn't matter how it ended." Yoshinobu said. "What matters is why are you in Japan to begin with."

"I was only here to study to country's history, nothing more." Kane said. "Why else would I be in Japan."

"Why did you destroy our Shogun undead?' Yoshinobu said.

"Excuse me?" Kane said. "What do you mean by your Shogun undead? You created those things?"

"We have such objects that can do a lot of things." Yoshinobu said.

"We created them for a future military run. Today's event was only a test run, which your actions came along and destroyed them."

"You have no reason for creating zombies." Kane said. "What more could they do for you or your military."

"We can do so much more for our military." Yoshinobu said. "We've been doing very much so."

"I hope you and your country are enjoying your time in the sun. Because as soon as I get out of here, I'm exposing your plot and your reign will fall."

Yoshinobu smirked and began walking towards the door.

"We'll see about that, Mr. Kane. If you can escape this room anyway."

Yoshinobu leaves the room and locked the door. Kane turned his head towards the door behind him. He begins to move his arms around to let them loose. After moving left and right, he releases his left arm and lowers it towards his left leg. Reaching into his boot, he pulled out a blade and cut the rope from his arms and legs. Kane stands up and walked to the door. He tried to open it, though the door wouldn't bulge. Kane shoves his shoulder into the door three times. The door does not even move. Kane decides to pull out a small sharp knife from his coat pocket and jams it into the crack of the door. After shoving it through, the door opened as Kane jumped out of the room. He sees he's in a hallway covered with red, green, and white Japanese art and paintings.

"Which way should I go?" Kane said.

Kane chooses to head left in the hallway, passing by closed doors that could be a room like the interrogation room he was previously locked into. He turned down the hallway and quickly stopped as he seen two soldiers guarding a gate that leads into the other side of the castle. Kane slowly slips through the guards and finds himself entering the Shogun army base. He scans the interior of the base, noticing all the army's weapons and armor. Passing by one of the tables of weapons, he discovers two circular blades that look like two shrunken. He sees they have handles on the back as he pulled them, the blades quickly turn with a loud buzzing sound. Kane releases the handles and smiles.

"What a great invention."

Kane takes the blades and looked forward, seeing another door. He opened the door and sees numerous dead Shogun soldiers laying on beds and laboratory tables. Kane scans the bodies and notice their veins are glowing a greenish color. Kane's eyes squint as if he's seen the liquid before. He looks on the right side of the room, seeing a blanket covering a large object. Kane yanked the cover sheet off the object, revealing it.

"It makes sense now." Kane said. "Perfect sense."

Kane paused as he stared at a destroyed and somewhat damaged alien spacecraft. He walked over to touch the object but notices the green liquid that surrounds it. He backed up and looked at the bodies again, doing the math in his head, he realizes that the spacecraft liquid was used on dead soldiers to resurrect them as zombies. Kane searches the room to find a way to release the ship from its connection to the wall as its pumping the liquid into the dozen bodies of soldiers.

"How do I release this object from this wall?"

Kane reached to his right side and pulled out his sword and tries to swipe the long cable that its connected to the spacecraft to the wall. The sword doesn't leave any sort of mark on the cable. Kane pulled out two knives and tries to stab the cable from the wall. Not making any improvement as he tried jamming the knives in between the cable and the wall, Kane finally decided to use the Edo Blades. As he swiped the cable with left and right attacks, the cable suddenly gives loose, snatching itself from the wall as the spacecraft leaned and fell to the ground, causing a great disturbance to the soldiers standing outside the base.

Kane heard the footsteps of the soldiers entering the base and heading closer to the door. He searched the room for a way out and finds a small door to the right of the room hidden by a dirty brown curtain. He leaves out through the door just as the soldiers enter. Seeing the spacecraft on the ground and the cable cut from the wall, they sound the alarm. Kane tries to escape the castle's premises as he ran faster than he could possibly think. Though, he found himself surrounded by more Shogun soldiers, with Yoshinobu behind them.

"You thought you could easily escape my grips."

"It was worth a shot. Just wanted to see what you would do."

Yoshinobu looked at his soldiers. He nodded towards them and turned back toward Kane.

"Men, bring Mr. Kane to the dojo."

The soldiers snatch Kane by his arms and pull him into the dojo arena. They toss Kane in the middle of the room, facing Yoshinobu. Kane gets to his feet and sees he's surrounded by over a dozen soldiers, standing guard with their swords in hand. He looked at Yoshinbou, who's getting out of his robe, wearing a somewhat form of militaristic-martial-arts uniform. He grabbed his sword from the wall and approached Kane.

"I'll give you a chance. If you can defeat me in battle, I will let you leave the castle grounds and you can be on your way out of Japan."

"Very well. If that's what you want."

Kane stands face to face with Shogun Yoshinobu. Both have their swords drawn, facing each other. They began to circle each other as the Shogun soldiers stood still. Yoshinobu started to smirk at Kane, causing him to question the uncertainty of the battle.

"Well, are you ready to fall?"

"Only if you make the first move."

Yoshinobu swiped a rough swing toward Kane with his sword. Kane jumped back and slowly paused while he stared into Yoshinobu's deadly eyes. Kane moved slowly as he circled Yoshinobu, who did the same. The soldiers continued to surround them without making any moves or sounds. Kane turned to one soldier, who's holding a French rifle and swiped his arm, cutting it off.

"They won't even move." Kane said.

Yoshinobu jumped toward Kane with the sword in front. Kane swiped the sword with his own. Knocking it to the ground, Yoshinobu picked it up and raised the sword in the air, coming down like a strike of lightning. Kane held his sword up, blocking the impact of Yoshinobu. Kane struggled to hold back Yoshinobu's impressive physical strength. Kane noticed he was going down toward his knees as he couldn't fight off Yoshinbou's strength. He pushed back, slowly rising above Yoshinobu. As he faced Yoshinobu in the face, he kicked him in the abdomen, knocking him back.

"You decide to use your own body?" Yoshinobu said.

"In a fight, you use all that you have."

Yoshinobu dropped his sword and kicked it toward the wall. He began to set up in a pose as Kane stared. Yoshinobu moved swiftly as he kicked Kane in the face, knocking him into the soldiers. Which the soldiers shoved Kane back towards Yoshinobu, who proceeded to pummel Kane with various martial arts techniques of punches and kicks. Yoshinobu raised his elbow up above Kane's back and slammed it down. Kane fell to the ground in massive pain. Spitting out blood, he laid on the cold and hard wooden floor as he looked at Yoshinobu standing above him with his sword.

"It would seem you're not a great fighter, Mr. Kane. To which you appear to be much weaker than what the stories have told."

Yoshinobu raised the sword above Kane's throat. As he drove the sword toward Kane, he moved and kicked Yoshinobu from behind, knocking him through the window and outside. The soldiers began to move towards the window. Jumping through it and going to the outside, Kane proceeded to follow them. While outside, Yoshinobu noticed that most of Edo's civilians were standing by, staring at their Shogun. He yelled at them in Japanese to return to their homes. Kane jumped out of the window behind Yoshinobu. The civilians were covered with fear as they stared at Kane.

"So, you want to continue this battle?" Yoshinobu said.

"I plan on defeating you in front of your own people. To show them that even a leader of a country falls."

Yoshinobu ran toward Kane. Making a variety of attacks toward him. Kane dodged the attacks and backhanded Yoshinobu, who turned around as he held the right side of his face. He rubbed his lips, seeing blood on his hand. He turned to Kane with a fire in his eyes and he ran back toward him. He continued the attacks toward Kane. Getting a few jabs and haymakers in on Kane, Kane kicked Yoshinobu in the stomach and punched him in the face, knocking him to the pavement. Kane looked up at the civilians and turned to the soldiers.

"This is your Emperor."

As the civilians stared, an abrupt sound of distant groans began to approach their location. Civilians began to run as a horde of zombies approached the location. The Shogun soldiers ran over and began fighting off the horde. Swiping their heads and arms off with their swords and firing at them from a distance with their rifles. Other soldiers were ambushed by the zombies. Two zombies spot Kane and Yoshinobu. As they approach, Kane went back into the dojo, picked up his sword and ran back through the shattered window and began cutting off the heads of the zombies. Yoshinobu looked up and seen the horde of zombies against his soldiers, as well as Kane fighting a few of them off. He got back to his feet as Kane turned toward him.

"What are you staring at, Yoshinobu? Aren't you going to fight?"

Yoshinobu didn't say a word and walked back into the dojo. Kane shook his head as he continued to fight off the rest of the zombies. Many of the soldiers were killed by the zombies or by the green liquid that dripped from their decayed bodies. After the fight, Kane returned into Edo Castle and grabbed whatever was left of his gear and decided to leave Japan.


Upon leaving Japan, the following year, Kane discovered that Yoshinobu had retired from being the Shogun of Japan and wasn't seen by anyone of the public eye again. He also found out that it was the last and final Shogun, thus making it the end of Feudal Japan.

# THE DEVILS AND THE DEMONS

## 1870
# VICTORIAN ERA

In the middle of the year 1870, Monster Hunter and Ufologist Gabriel Kane walked into the lair to have a meeting with the Knights of the *Symbolum Venatores*, the Order of Hunters. Once inside the large conference room, covered in memorabilia of hunters throughout the ages, they sat. Kane sat with the Order as they discussed their new plan to him. The Order requested for Kane to end a group that is called The Cult. Kane asked them more about the group, figuring out how they worked and what they've done to others that have crossed their path. The Order told Kane The Cult are a group of Satan worshippers who have committed various murders across Europe and have been involved in Satanic rituals of both human and animal sacrifices.

Kane agreed to find the group and annihilate them off the earth. As he walked out of the room, they warn him to be very careful of apparent demons that follow them in the shadows as well as their strength, a gift due to their high worshipping. Kane stated he'll take his chances and headed off onto his quest.

Kane traveled to the eastern side of England, searching for The Cult. Showing no signs of the satanic group, Kane decided to travel to the northern area of England. Kane traveled almost nonstop searching for The Cult.

Nightfall caught up to Kane and the sun's light dimmed away. Kane pulled out a lamp to see where he's walking. His coat and hat stood out as his silhouette shown through the shadows and the wind was slightly blowing.

"There has to be some way of finding this group before complete darkness covers the lands."

While moving, he heard sudden sounds of footsteps are heard around Kane. He slowly reaches for his pistol and aims it around him. The footsteps are getting closer.

"Whoever you are, I suggest you reveal yourself." Kane said.

Kane continued to hear the footsteps around him as the sound appears to come closer. Kane reached to his other pistols and holds it up along with the other pistol. He circles himself around the location as he begins to see cloaked figures circling him. Dressed in all black robes with hoods covering their faces. They're not making and noises of any kind, except for their creepy footsteps. Kane glanced back at the entire crowd before one of the cloaked figures approached him directly. Kane holds the pistol towards the cloaked figure's forehead.

"State your names immediately!" Kane said. "Before I have to just rid you off before me and continue on my journey."

"We are The Cult."

"Cult of what? Wizards? Demons?"

"We are The Cult of Hastur, our Fallen Angel and Savior."

"Hastur? The Fallen demon."

"He is our Angel and our Savior! You will speak of him not. Until you become a member of his Cult."

"That will never cease to happen."

"Be that as it may. For we and Hastur know who you are. Gabriel Kane, the monster hunter and ufologist."

Kane smirked and cocked his head slightly while holding his pistols toward the Cult around him.

"So, you know who I am. I take it that Hastur sent you here to stop me from finding you and killing you all."

"Hastur warned us or a coming force that rides in the night to stop his works as well as ours. We will not stand by and let you destroy what our savior has created and built for us. For he has spoken and has declared that we vanquish you off the face of earth, so that he can continue his work for his coming rule."

"If what you're saying is true and your boss wants me dead. Why don't you and your guys take care of me now while I'm still here by myself."

"Don't worry. We're about to."

The cloaked figure turned around facing the Cult. He raised up his hand and lowered it in the direction of Kane. He turned toward Kane and revealed his eyes. A piercing red glow emits from them as Kane pointed both pistols toward him.

"What the hell are you people."

"We're worshippers of Hastur. He's given us power that many humans cease to believe in our time and later in the future generation. Until our savior returns and turns this world into his own kingdom of chaos and death."

"Not while I'm still around."

Kane fired a shot to the cloaked figure's head. The bullet goes through his head as he fell to the ground. The Cult looked down at his body and raised their heads toward Kane in complete silence.

"Anyone up for the next round?" Kane said.

The Cult ran toward Kane as he fired shots continuously around him. Blowing off heads and shooting through abdomens. The Cult reached closer as Kane placed his pistols back into their holsters and took out a sword. Kane began slicing through the Cult as they came closer toward him. One member of the Cult slapped Kane in the face. Kane smiled and cut the head off the member. Kane continued fighting off the Cult and discovered their seemly increasing in numbers.

"How are they doing this."

Kane found himself being smothered by The Cult, until a blast of light appears from behind him. The Cult look up toward the light and immediately covered their faces as the light burned them. The Cult ran off into the darkness of the nearby forests as Kane was crouched on the ground, covering his head. After a brief of silence, Kane stood up and looked around, not seeing any of the Cult in sight. He looked behind him and seen a man standing, facing him. The man wore a suit and had a moustache and short black hair. Kane took a greater look at the man as he closed a book he was holding before placing it into his pocket.

"I suggest you say something. That way I know you're not possessed and in control of your own self." The man said. "So, I won't have to kill you."

"I recognize you from somewhere. I may ask who you are?"

"We might have cross paths once, for starters. But, allow me to introduce or reintroduce myself. My name is Thomas Carnacki."

"The Thomas Carnacki. The Ghost-Finder."

"Correct, Mr. Gabriel Kane."

Kane and Carnacki stare down each other as they meet for the very first time. Kane placed his sword back into his holder as Carnacki stood still.

"How do you know my name?"

"There are so many tales that concern you, Mr. Kane. Many describe who you are and what you've done throughout your illustrious history."

"So, I take that I can ask what you are doing out here?"

"I'm looking for a being that's known as Hastur. A fallen demon of sorts. I had understood that a group called The Cult were his army or worshippers that gave him the power to do the things that he wished."

"You just ran them off with your light sorcery."

Carnacki waived his hand toward Kane while he shook his head.

"I possess no sorcery of any kind. I've trained in many ways that I've learn how to use the energy that lives around us in our everyday lives."

"Be that as you say, I'll rather use my weapons to get the job done. That way it's a clean kill."

"Seems that you do not have much faith in using the energies of this world."

"I have faith. Only not in those who decide to use other means to fight their battles for them."

"If you believe your words so. Why are you out here exactly? If I may ask. For investigation purposes."

"I'm also on the hunt for Hastur and I found The Cult. Had them in my grasp before you arrived and ran them off.

"They nearly had you on the ground to rip your body apart for the worshipping. I came along and saved your life here. So, I suggest you show someone like me a little respect and say thank you."

Kane walked up toward Carnacki and looked him in the eyes.

"You'll get your respect when I receive my respect."

Carnacki nodded with a smile.

"We'll see how you'll get your respect, Mr. Kane. Until then, we'll travel together to find Hastur. Remember, two hands are better than one."

"We'll see how your work will pay off. This isn't some ordinary ghost that you're dealing with. This is a demonic force that preys on fear and hopes on gaining control of the world as we know it."

"I know what we're dealing with and I will handle it accordingly to how I do my work. As for you, just do what you know how to do and don't get in my way when we come across Hastur and his Cult."

Carnacki walked off into the forest as Kane looked on. He reached down and picked his hat up from off the ground and placed it back onto his head.

"The suggestion is the same here, Carnacki."

Kane walked into the forest behind Carnacki. Holding his pistols in hand as Carnacki continued to carry his book throughout their walk in the forest. Carnacki looked back and nodded his head.

"So, how many things have you come across in your lifetime of being a hunter?"

"I've come across things that the world disbelieves. Many of those things include the undead, extraterrestrials, mummies, spirits, and so on."

"So, you've never come across a werewolves or vampires?"

"I have yet to encounter such creatures. I know I will in the future, but for now, my focus is on finding Hastur and stopping him and his cult of crazed mortals."

While walking through the forest, they find a spot in the middle of the forest where no trees stood tall and hardly any bushes or high grass was settled. Carnacki walked over toward the cleared spot and kneeled. He reached and rubbed the ground and sniffed his hand.

"Smells like this area was burned by something."

Kane walked over and sniffed the ground. Taking a second to think, he slowly reached for his pistols.

"It's sulfur."

Kane looked up and in front of him and spotted a horde of demons. All with sharp teeth and claws that smelled like brimstone on their darkened scaled bodies. Kane shoved Carnacki as he glanced up toward the demons.

"Oh dear." Carnacki said. "What shall we do about them?"

"What do you think. We'll fight them all off and clear this area."

Kane ran toward them as he fired shots from his pistols. Killing a few of the demons as Carnacki took out his book and began reciting rituals against the demons that threw them off of what they sought out to do. Kane took out his sword and sliced through the demons. He glanced back as Carnacki who was reading out of his book.

"Carnacki! What the hell are you doing over there!"

"Patience, Mr. Kane. For I am about to save our lives at this moment in an instant."

"We'll see who saved who."

Carnacki began reading from the book and immediately the demos started to vanish completely. Kane looked around as the demons disappeared through a thick black smoke. As they vanished by numbers, Kane looked over toward Carnacki, who held his book in the air and continued reciting the ritual. Once he completed the ritual, the demons were vanished completely from the entire area. Kane walked over toward Carnacki and took one glance at the book.

"What the hell is in that book of yours?"

"Words that will save our lives for this purpose of saving this world."

"If you say."

"Let's continue on searching for our leading quests."

Carnacki and Kane continued walking through the forest. While walking, Kane could hear something rustling around in the trees above them. The sound was intense enough to the point that Kane began firing shots into the trees. Carnacki turned and looked back at Kane.

"What are you doing?"

"Whatever is in the trees is too big for an animal."

"For God's sake, its only animals running around in those trees.

Nothing more could it be."

Carnacki took one step further, a member of the Cult jumped down from the trees in front of Carnacki and smacked him through the trees and into another large tree trunk. Kane looked and reached for his pistol before being snatched and thrown across the trees.

"You individuals will never cease to understand the power of our savior, Hastur. For he is great to us as we are to him."

"I'm tired of hearing what you believe about your demon."

Kane lunged toward the member and punched her, knocking her on the ground. Carnacki gets to his feet and approached Kane. Wiping the dirt and moss of his coat, Carnacki looked down at the member and recognized it was a woman. He looked at Kane.

"Tell me you didn't hit a woman."

"She attacked me first. She deserved it for being a worshipper of a demon."

They began to hear footsteps coming from behind them. Crushing fallen branches with each step. Kane and Carnacki turned around facing the entire Cult. All of which had glowing red eyes. Kane pulled out his pistols as Carnacki reached for his book.

"You've come too far to ruin our savior's work. Now, we have choice but to kill the two of you and sacrifice your bodies and your blood to Hastur, our savior."

"Not today." Kane said.

Kane fired shots, though the bullets went through the Cult completely. Not even leaving a mark of any kind. Kane paused as he looked over to Carnacki, who began turning pages in his book as the Cult ran toward them.

"Carnacki, they're approaching us."

"One moment, Gabriel Kane. I'm searching for something here."

"We don't have time to do this, Carnacki."

"Just have patience this once, young one."

The Cult inched closer toward them as Kane held his sword in front. He glanced at Carnacki who continued turning pages. Kane began to become enraged at Carnacki's actions.

"CARNACKI!!! DO YOUR WORK!!!"

"If you insist so greatly."

Carnacki opened the book to the point of which the book could nearly be ripped in half if it opened more. He began reading what he called the Sigsand Manuscript. The Cult had suddenly stopped and looked at their bodies. Carnacki glanced over toward Kane.

"Fire your shots, Mr. Kane. Before this ritual runs off."

"If you say."

Kane fired shots from his pistols and immediately began killing the members of the Cult. He continued firing as he thought to himself what exactly is Carnacki dealing with within that book of his. Nearly running out of ammo, Kane decided to use his sword and began cutting through the Cult completely from every angle he could possibly picture in his mind. It finally came down to the last three members of the Cult in which they ran toward Kane and Carnacki. Carnacki dodged a punch and slammed the member to the ground before stomping on his chest. Kane ducked the shots from the other two and sliced them both in half. He looked down at the other one and stabbed it in its hearts as Carnacki looked on.

"I didn't suspect you had any physical fight within you."

"I prefer to use my book to get the jobs done rather than my fists and feet."

Kane turned around and noticed a building nearby. He pointed in the direction as he and Carnacki walked over toward the area. Once they reached the area, Kane realizes it's a church. He also spots significant symbols and lettering around the church's walls and notices that a cross that sits atop the church is upside down.

"Appears we've found their worshipping site."

"Seems you are correct on that statement, Mr. Kane."

They approached the door and Kane kicked in the doors. As both walk inside the church, they discover a large amount of animal skins laying around the walls of the church and they also noticed a strong odor of blood within the church's walls.

"I take it you smell the blood." Kane said.

"I surely smell it."

"Now, we need to see what's in here to stop Hastur."

They walk near the altar before hearing a sudden rumbling sound coming from underneath them, near the altar.

"What is going on?" Carnacki said.

"It's him."

The floor blows open, knocking Kane and Carnacki to the ground in the aisle. They can only see dirt flying in the air. Kane fans his arms, moving the dirt from his sight. As the dirt and dust cleared from the air, they found themselves staring at Hastur himself. A large demon with rough burned skin, ram-like horns, and bones on his back that resembled wings.

"I've finally come to terms of seeing my Cult couldn't rid you off this decadent wasteland."

"So, you're Hastur. The fallen demon that's come to rule over the lands." Kane said.

"I am that and much more. More of which you couldn't possibly understand with your human minds."

Kane and Carnacki continued to stare at Hastur. Staring at his large physique and his towering height of which nears the height of a grizzly bear on its hind legs. Kane pulled out his sword and pointed toward Hastur, who smiled.

"I do not know what you're smiling about, demon. Your end has finally come and has come to your own doorstep."

"The two of you combined don't have the strength or willpower to defeat me all on your own."

"You have no idea what kind of power we possess, Hastur. Many will remember this night greatly as the night the fallen demon Hastur met his death."

"We shall see whose death will culminate on this very night. One thing is highly sure, it won't be my death."

Hastur rammed at great force with impressive speed into both Kane and Carnacki, shoving them into the concrete walls of the church. Both struggled to let themselves free from Hastur's rough horns.

Kane began stabbing Hastur in both his abdomen and back with his sword. Hastur roared in pain as he backed away from Kane and Carnacki. Carnacki tried to regain his breath as Kane ran over toward Hastur and continued stabbing the large demon in his abdomen. Hastur swiped his arm across Kane, who ducked and went behind him, stabbing him in his back. Hastur raised his foot up and back kicked Kane into the wall.

"Weak mortal. You believe giving me mild pain from a metal blade will end my existence."

"I'm trying what I believe has a chance to work against a being such as yourself."

"Just accept your death as a favor of my gratitude."

While Hastur started walking toward Kane as he reached onto his side, pulling out from his coat a double-barred shotgun. Hastur stopped and stared at the weapon. Preferably into the barrels.

"Guess I'll give this a try." Kane said.

Kane fired the shotgun, blasting Hastur on his chest, blowing him back a few steps. Hastur was appalled by the force of the shotgun and looked at his chest. Rubbing it before looking down at Kane. Only black and reddish ash fell from Hastur's chest. It even smelled of a greater sulfur mixed with the gunpowder. Carnacki looked on as he turned pages through his book.

"That weapon you possess has great power. Yet it fails to have the power to finish me off."

"I haven't used it to its full potential."

Kane fired another shot that blew off one of Hastur's horns. He roared in massive pain to where Kane and Carnacki covered their ears to protect them from any damage due to the loud road. Hastur shook his head and his eyes began to glow a dark red emitting smoke from them.

"I've toiled with you humans enough! Now I finish you completely."

Hastur reached down as Kane took another shot, shooting a small hole through Hastur's right hand. He smirked as he jerked Kane by his coat and held him up to the equal height of himself. Hastur stared into Kane's eyes as he began talking in an unusual way. Carnacki looked on and stopped on one page.

"He's trying to possess Kane."

Carnacki ran over toward Hastur, who spotted Carnacki and swiped him back against the wall. Hastur looked back toward Kane and smiled.

"If you shall not perish, I shall make you one of my own. Someone with your skill set will be very useful for my ruling army in the days to come.”

“Your days won’t be coming, Hastur.” Carnacki said. “For your days are done away with as I read this ritual to send you back into your prison.”

Hastur threw Kane to the wall as he ran over toward Carnacki, who read the ritual aloud. Hastur noticed that his body was degrading in front of him. He looked down at Carnacki as he continued to yell out the ritual.

“No! Stop what you’re doing, mortal. Stop!”

“I now send you back into your prison for all eternity.”

Hastur’s body completely falls apart as he turned to black smoke before a bright light appeared out of the book and approached the smoke as it inhaled it completely as it disappeared. The church is silent as Kane gets to his feet and nodded at Carnacki.

“Great job.” Kane said.

“Same goes to you, Mr. Kane.”

The church began to rumble as it started to fall apart. Kane and Carnacki ran out of the church as it fell to the ground and became nothing but dust and debris. They took one last look at the demolished church before facing each other.

“Seems the job is done.” Carnacki said.

“For now.”

“Until we meet again in this matter.”

“That’s what I was thinking.”

They shook hands. Ending their recent partnership as they walked their separate ways, leaving the church completely abandoned in the middle of the forest.


Several days later, Kane returned to the Order, where they thanked him for stopping Hastur. Kane replied to them how he had assistance in his quest to which the Order stopped him from continuing and mentioned that Carnacki was given their blessings for helping. Kane stood silent as he stared at the Order.

“How did you know Carnacki was aligned with me?”

"Because we sent him. We know you're still a young man who's learning his steps in this new life, so we thought we should send someone who's well-trained in this field of the supernatural."

"You could've at least said something to the extent of him investigating the same incidents."

As they spoke with each other, Carnacki had walked through the doors as he handed the Order a scroll. They nodded to him as he glanced at Kane and nodded. Kane nodded back as Carnacki left the room. The Order placed the scroll on the table before speaking to Kane.

"Still, you've done your job and it has done us greatly."

"If there's anything out there that might need my hand involved, you know how to contact me."

Kane left the Order's lair and stood outside, watching the sun arose from behind the clouds.

# THE HOWL OF THE WOLFMAN

## 1877
# LONDON

England has been on the rough end of murders throughout the past few weeks. Witnesses have reported over a dozen killings that were apparently caused by a "Wolfman". The police have been on the series of murders for weeks and haven't found a trace. Now, they have decided to contact Gabriel Kane to investigate these Wolfman murders. After three days, Kane arrived in London, starting his search for the Wolfman.


Kane headed into the London City Police Headquarters. When he entered the building, the people turned to him, automatically knowing he's the Monster Hunter and Ufologist known across the world. Kane walked toward an officer standing by the lobby counter.

"The commissioner of your city wanted to see me." Kane said to a officer.

"Yes, Mr. Kane." The officer said. "His office is right down that hall."

Kane looked down the hall, gazing at the newspaper clippings on the walls, all focused on the Wolfman sightings and murders. Kane saw a door in front of him and entered the room. Inside is the commissioner of the police sitting at his desk. Kane knocked on the door.

"Who's there?" The commissioner asked.

"Gabriel Kane." Kane said. "The man you've contacted."

The commissioner raised his head up from the desk, covered with paper, staring at Kane. He welcomed him into the office. Kane sat in the chair facing the commissioner.

"I'm truly glad you could make it." The commissioner said.

"I go where I'm needed." Kane said.

"We needed you here because of your certain background with these types of investigations." The commissioner said. "We've received reports that the series of murders that have been caused over the past few weeks were done by a werewolf or Wolfman as the witnesses call it."

"I've heard of such a beast, but never encountered one. What location have these murders occurred?"

The commissioner revealed a map of the city from his desk drawer. He laid it out on the desk, Kane glanced over it as the commissioner pointed to the location.

"Right here, in the City Park." The commissioner said. "Most of the murders have occurred at this site. Others were in the woods and two in an alleyway just across town."

"Any traces of a suspect?" Kane asked. "Just to be sure?"

"There haven't been any signs of a suspect. Nor any traces."

"Here, I will help you on this investigation." Kane said. "Get to the bottom of it."

"I thank you for that, Mr. Kane." The commissioner said.

While Kane prepared to leave, another man entered the office. The man has curly black hair and he's wearing a black frock coat with an upturned collar shirt, a brown silk waistcoat, and black slacks with brown dress shoes. The commissioner stood up to approach the man, shaking his hand. The man later turned his attention toward Kane, who walked toward him.

"Kane, I like you to meet Mr. Sherlock Holmes." The commissioner said. "He'll also be on this investigation as well."

"The well-known Sherlock Holmes." Kane said. "An honor to meet you."

The two detectives shook hands.

"You're the great Gabriel Kane." Holmes said. "The Monster Hunter/Ufologist. Let me ask a question. What's a Ufologist, really?"

"This isn't the time for questions. We're on a serious investigation and I'll like to get to it."

Kane leaves the office as Holmes and the commissioner look back at him.

"He's got quite the temper." Holmes gestured.

"He takes his job very serious, Mr. Holmes. I hope you do the same on this case."

"Don't worry about it, Commissioner. I'm highly excited for this case. Its about a Wolfman."

Outside, Kane gets onto his horse and rode off, looking at a map of the city. He begins the investigation by heading towards London City Park. Holmes walked outside of the police headquarters, taking note of Kane riding off in the distance.

"Impatient one I'm guessing." Holmes said as he gets onto his horse and follows Kane.

Kane rode through the city of London toward the City Park, Holmes came over on the side of him. Kane took a quick glance over at him with uncertainty.

"How would someone like you be a part of this particular case?" Kane asked.

"Because, I can solve any case. Ordinary or supernatural. I can get the job done."

"I hope so." Kane remarked.

"By the way, my partner, Dr. Watson will be joining us. He should meet us at the City Park."

"I'm not a fan of being in the crowd. Much less a fan of anything."

They reached the City Park and began their search. Kane took to the eastern portion of the park while Holmes searched the western portion. Civilians stared at Kane, due to his well-known background. He approached one male civilian.

"Excuse me, sir, have you seen anything unusual in this park?"

"No. Nothing." The civilian answered.

"Thanks."

On the other side of the park, Holmes continued his search for clues as he flirted with a pair of women walking through the park. As he flirted, Dr. John H. Watson, wearing his casual slacks and vest coat with a brown coachman's hat, approached from behind.

"What exactly are you doing, Holmes?"

"What does it look like?" Holmes said. "I'm speaking with these beautiful women here. But I'm glad you've arrived to help."

"Help with what? You're flirting techniques or this Werewolf case?"

The women look at Holmes, questioning him about the Wolfman case. He grinned, enjoying and savoring the women' attention. Holmes continued speaking with the women as Kane walked up behind the women.

"This isn't the time for messing around." Kane declared with certainty.

"Just relax. Here, meet Dr. Watson."

Kane glanced at Watson and shook his hand.

"It's good to meet you."

"Indeed." Watson said. "What have you discovered so far?"

"Nothing. Haven't found a clue."

Holmes looked to Kane and Watson. Smiling.

"I think it's best we return later tonight and investigate." said Holmes. "Since the murders only occurred during the night."

"Agreed." Watson said.

"Good thinking." Kane remarked. "At least you're using your mind this once."

Kane leaves the park as Holmes looks back at Watson.

"He doesn't like me very much, does he." Holmes said.

"You can't tell, Holmes." Watson said.


Kane, Holmes, and Watson return to the City Park later that night and its completely dark and quiet. The only thing they can hear is the sound of crickets and their horses as the snow falls from the sky. They walk together, not splitting up, though that's what Kane wants to do. Holmes look at the sky, towards the moon. He sees the clouds covering it.

"They say that this 'Wolfman' always appeared when there was a full moon." Holmes said.

"That is correct." Kane said. "Why do you ask?"

Holmes pointed towards the sky, as Kane and Watson look right above them. The clouds are covering a partly of the moon. They can't tell if it's a full moon or a crescent moon.

"Can't tell.' Holmes said. 'What do you guys think? I'm just observing it right now.'

"Judging by my view, it seems to be a crescent moon.' Watson said. 'If you look just towards the right, you can see the top point of the moon.'

"Really?' Holmes said. 'I don't see it.'

Kane looked towards the direction of Watson's. He turns back to Holmes.

"Just wait for the clouds to move over.' Kane said. 'Once that happens, we'll get a good view of the moon.'

"So, Kane, what types of cases have you been on before this one?' Holmes asked.

"I've done a few exorcisms, I also encountered a living mummy controlled by aliens nine years ago.' Kane said. 'When I was twenty-three, I was involved, well rather pulled along into the American Civil War while investigating an extraterrestrial crash site. I've encountered zombies, gargoyles, warlocks, and among other things.'

"You've basically been through hell and back over your lifetime.' Watson said.

"Pretty much.' Kane replied. 'It's what keeps me going.'

Holmes and Watson discuss the moon to each other, Kane notices something in the bushes towards the left of them. He slowly walks over to the bushes, with his right hand to his side, slowly grabbing hold of his pistol. Watson notices Kane moving slowly and so does Holmes.

"He's found something.' Watson said.

"I wonder what exactly?' said Holmes. 'There has to be something around here with a clue.'

Kane reached closer to the bushes and pulls out the pistol, aiming it into the bushes. He looks around it and sees a brown cat jump from the bushes, running into the darkness. Kane looks on as Holmes and Watson come from behind him.

"It was only a cat it seems.' said Holmes.

"At least he debunked it.' Watson replied.

Kane moved toward them, looking up and noticed the clouds have moved, unveiling a full moon. He then sees something huge, standing a few feet behind Holmes and Watson. He sees it has a long snout, long high ears, the claws on its hands and feet, and its body covered completely in brown fur. Kane has finally seen the Wolfman.

"Move!" Kane yelled. "It's behind you!"

Turning around, facing the Wolfman. Howling and pouncing toward them on all fours. Holmes and Watson raised up their revolvers and begin firing at the Wolfman. Kane reached into his left side, pulling out silver bullets, reloading his pistols.

"Why aren't our shots working?" Holmes asked.

"You need silver bullets?!" Kane yelled.

Holmes turns to Watson, no sign of expression on his face. Watson looks at Holmes, while still firing at the Wolfman.

"We don't have silver bullets, do we?" Holmes wondered with confusion.

This is not the time!' Watson said.

Kane finished reloading and fires at the Wolfman. It swiftly moves side to side, avoiding the shots. It looks down and notices the silver bullets. It looks up at the three and roars, before running into the darkness of the park.

"Damn it! Where did it go?!"

Holmes takes out a flashlight and points it towards the darker area of the park. He notices something moving around. He starts running toward the darker area.

"There it is!" Holmes said. "Right down here!"

"Be careful, Holmes!" Kane yelled. "It can be a trap!"

"Don't worry yourself, Mr. Kane. I know what I'm doing."

Holmes, walked through the dark area, hearing rumbling throughout the bushes around him. He looked around, not seeing anything. Holmes turned back toward Kane and Watson. They glanced at him, questioning.

"There's nothing here." Holmes said. "It must've run off."

"You sure?" Watson asked.

"I'm positive There's nothing here."

Kane ran over to Holmes, looking both left and right for the Wolfman. He gets to Holmes and searches the area himself. Holmes only stares at Kane.

"You really had to look for yourself, I see.' Holmes said. 'I just said there's nothing over here.'

"Over here, yes. But, what about over there."

Kane points to the left of the area, facing the exit to the park. Standing by the exit is a man, whose only wearing torn pants. Kane runs over to the man, as Holmes and Watson follow. Once they reach the man, they notice that he's out of breath.

"What's his problem?"

"Have to find out."

Kane attempted to grab the man's attention, but nothing worked. Holmes knelt in front of the man, staring into his shocked eyes.

"Excuse me, sir." said Holmes. "Have you seen a Wolfman anywhere?"

The man slowly turns his head toward Holmes, facing him. The man starts to sob as if he's both sad and afraid.

"Wolfman?" The man uttered loudly. "There's no Wolfman here."

Kane's temper starts to get the better of him as he gets into the man's face, aiming his pistol towards the man's forehead, staring a hole deeply through him. Holmes looks at Kane and backs off, standing next to Watson.

"Now tell me, have you seen this creature?" Kane asked the man. "Have you seen it?"

"No!" The man yelled. "I haven't seen a Wolfman!"

Holmes looked at the moon, the clouds have shaded its light. He tapped Kane on his left shoulder, pointing up.

"If the moon's cover, does it stay a werewolf, or does it change back into a human?" Holmes questioned.

Kane gazed above him at the shrouded moon, turning back towards the man.

"Him." Kane said. "He's the Wolfman."

"Really?" Holmes asked. "Because he's looks a little slim to be a gruesome beast."

"It's him!' Kane yelled. "Watch the clouds, for when they move, he'll turn back into the werewolf."

Kane pulled out both pistols, aiming them towards the man, Holmes does the same and Watson looked up at the moon, the clouds started to fade away, revealing the full moon once again.

"The clouds are gone." Watson said.

"Cover me." Kane yelled.

They backed up, watching the man. Within seconds, they noticed him starting to twitch. He cramped up into a cradle on the ground, holding himself in his arms. As he screamed in pain, the tone in his voice decreased in pitch. Growing deeper, beast-like. He glared toward them.

"Run for your lives, gentlemen. RUN!"

The man's skin starts to peel off his body like dead shreds of hair. Beneath the shredding skin, thick brown hair starts to grow in its place. The man's head transforms painfully into a snout as he ears heighten. His eyes change from green to yellow. His nails transform into sharp razor claws as his hands and feet turn completely hairy. The man turns toward them and reveals himself to be the Wolfman. He roared at them and lunged.

"Watson!' Kane yelled. "Watch out!"

Kane fired a shot toward the Wolfman's chest, straight into the heart. The Wolfman and Watson both fell to the ground after the fire.

"John!" Holmes yelled. "Are you alright?!"

They helped Watson to his feet, dusting the dirt off his shoulders. He looks at them, holding his right side.

"I'm ok. Just a bruise will remain. Nothing dire."

"That's a good thing you didn't get bit." Kane said. "Otherwise, that could've been you later."

Placing the pistols back onto his sides, Kane approached the Wolfman's body, realizing he's transformed back into human form and dead.

"Looks like we're done here." Holmes said. "Who wants a drink? I know I do."

"Indeed. This was something I never studied for."

"Not many in your fields have study such truths." Kane said. "*Requiescat in Pace.*"

The next morning, Kane returned to the police headquarters as the entire city of London thanked him, Holmes, and Watson for finding and killing the Wolfman. They thanked the city and Kane's work was finished. His focus was set to leave London, heading off into the western side of Europe. Outside, Holmes came towards him.

"I only wanted to say that I appreciated the time we worked together."

"I have to say it's an honor to have worked with a famous detective." said Kane. "You take care and tell Watson that I said get well."

"I will." Holmes said. "Surely."

Kane rode off out of London, not even looking back to the city. Holmes prepared to leave when spotted Watson nowhere to be found. Inside a public bathroom, Watson is staring at himself in the mirror. As he removed a part of his clothing from his right side, he saw blood. When he fully removed his shirt, he knew he wasn't bumped or scratched by the Wolfman. He was bitten.

"No." This cannot be happening."

# JOURNEY TO TRANSYLVANIA

## 1887
# TRANSYLVANIA

Transylvania is a highly known location to the world. A place where people fear due to its known history of vampire tales. Now, in the mid-1800s, Gabriel Kane, a monster hunter and ufologist, highly known for his encounters with legendary beasts across the world. Kane is a man in his late forties, lean and gloomy, somewhat somber looking. His skin appeared pale with cold eyes. His face is shadowed by his hat. He is dressed entirely in black and is equipped with a weaponry that features a rapier, a dagger, a cutlass, a cross made of steel, and a pair of flintlock pistols.

The reason for Kane becoming a monster hunter and ufologist is the fact that he believes that he was abducted in his early days by extraterrestrials. Now, with that knowledge, Kane's main goal in life is to rid the world of all evil in both legendary and extraterrestrials.

Kane, who's now on the road, heading towards London. As he is heading there, he makes a stop upon Hertfordshire. Kane enters the small country town, seeing its residents and how they look at him with fear. Kane sees a small bar and enters it, leaving his bold black horse standing in front of the bar, tied to a pole. Kane walks into the bar, which is filled with mostly men and a few women. The people in the bar notice Kane and stare at him. Kane walks towards the bar and sits on a stool as the people continue to stare. Kane looks at the female bartender.

"May I have a glass of whiskey?' Kane asked the bartender.

The bartender pulls out the whiskey bottle and pours it into a glass and hands the glass to Kane. Kane takes the glass and begins drinking the whiskey. As the bartender turns to put the glass away, Kane grunts, getting her attention.

"Leave the bottle here.' Kane said. 'If you please.'

"Yes sir.' said the bartender as she leaves the bottle in front of Kane.

She leaves the bottle and from behind Kane comes two men, wearing Victorian clothing, with one wearing a hat. They each stand on both sides of Kane and they stare at him.

"So, you must be Gabriel Kane.' the Man with the hat said.' 'The monster hunter.'

"The ufologist, too.' the other man said. 'So, tell me, Kane. What actually is an ufologist?'

"Do I really need to speak with you.' Kane said.

"You do if your life depended on it.' the man in the hat said.

"Hmm.' Kane said. 'If my life depended on it.

The man in the hat taps Kane on his hat. Kane feels the vibration and quickly turns around and punches the man in the hat. Kane stands up, staring deeply at the other man. He runs outside the bar. Kane looks down at the man on the ground.

"You dropped your hat.' Kane said smiling.

Kane finishes his last glass of whisky and leaves the bar. Outside, he gets onto his horse and rides off into the forest, continuing his journey.

Kane arrives in London and heads for the church. Inside the church is the Priest, who knows Kane on a professional and personal manner. He hears a horse outside and from the door comes Kane.

"Didn't expect you so soon." The Priest said.

"When I'm on a journey, I arrive faster than expected.' Kane said. 'So, what do you have for me?"

The priest walks over into the office and leans toward the desk. On the desk is a scroll. He hands the scroll to Kane, who opens it and reads it.

"From the look of this scroll, it seems Dr. Jekyll is on the loose again.' Kane said.

"It appears so.' The priest said. 'He was last spotted here in London. Which is why I contacted you."

"You want me to catch Dr. Jekyll and bring him to justice.' Kane said. 'I can do that, no problem."

"But, there is a catch, Gabriel.' The priest said. 'Jekyll has been seen as his alter-ego, Mr. Hyde."

"That should make it more exciting for me." Kane said.

"According to the local reports, Jekyll has been using his other persona to terrorize homes." The priest said. 'He has also even killed local civilians as well as their animals, if they owned farms, of course."

"Don't worry, old friend.' Kane said. 'I can take care of Jekyll and his big ego."

Kane thanked the priest. Leaving the church.


Outside Kane looks at the scroll and heads for the first location, East London. The sun is now setting as Kane travels to East London, during that period, Kane ran into a large pack of wolves. He passes them quickly them, though they chase him and his horse. Kane pulls out his pistols and begins firing at the wolves. He only kills two as the other three run off into the nearby woods.

The sun set and the moon arose, Kane arrived in East London. As he enters the location, the streets and surrounding are all but noisy. Usually around nighttime, the location would be crowded with individuals who would go out and have a good time with one another. But, Kane believes that everyone is in their homes only to avoid Dr. Jekyll's other half. Kane continues going through the location. He then notices a poster on a brick wall.

He gets off his horse and walks to the wall. He looks at the poster and sees an illustration of Jekyll's other half, Mr. Hyde. it's a Wanted, Dead or Alive poster.

"So, that's what he looks like." Kane said.

As he read the description of Hyde and as he reads it, he hears a loud scream. He runs over to his horse to track down the scream.

Kane's horse runs quickly toward the screaming. When Kane arrives he sees a man and a woman, laying on the ground, dead. Kane looks at their bodies, searching for any bite marks or animal wounds. Instead he only finds what appears to be saliva, from an unknown creature. Kane takes a sample of it and heads off, saying a prayer to the deceased man and woman. As Kane goes around the area, he sees a man on the side of the road. Wearing what appears to be a robe, his head covered with a hood.

"Excuse me.' Kane said. 'Do you know where I can find Dr. Jekyll?"

The man continues to stand still and silent, only throwing rocks into the nearby bay.

Kane gets off his horse and walks toward the man.

"I asked you a question, sir." Kane said.

Kane grabs the man and he turns around. Kane backs up, noticing that the man has no face.

"What the hell are you?" Kane said.

The man runs to Kane and knocks him down. The man pounces on top of Kane, trying to bite his face it seems. Kane struggles to get the man off and pulls out his dagger and stabs the man in the neck. The man falls to Kane's side as Kane gets to his feet and pulls the dagger out. Kane kneels and looks at the man, checking his features. Kane's very confused.

"What are you?" Kane said.

Kane leaves the body there and continued. In front of him, he sees an old abandoned church. He leaves the horse in front of the church as he enters. Inside the church, which is very, very old. From the look of the church, it hasn't been used in decades, maybe centuries, depending on how old the building is. Kane walks slowly on the wooden floor. His footsteps can be heard throughout the entire church. He reaches the upper floor and sees a man, sitting in the corner. He's not wearing a shirt, so Kane can only see him from behind. Kane stops and looks.

"Excuse me." Kane said. "Who are you and why are you here?"

"Leave me alone." The individual said. "I have peace here."

"Doesn't seem so." Kane said. "Tell me your name."

The man stands up and turns around, facing Kane.

"I am Dr. Jekyll." The individual said. "I know who you are, Gabriel Kane."

Kane pauses.

"Well, you know why I'm here." Kane said.

"You've come to take me out." Jekyll said. "Or should I say, you've come to take my other half out."

Kane walks slowly toward Jekyll, hands above him.

"Dr. Jekyll, let's not bring your big friend in here with us." Kane said. "He would cause a lot of trouble and damage."

"Well, it's too bad, Gabriel Kane." Jekyll said smiling. "Because he's already here."

Kane grabs Jekyll's arm and Jekyll hits Kane, knocking him across the room. Kane looks up and sees Jekyll transforming into Mr. Hyde. Now, Kane is staring in the eyes of Hyde.

"It's about time that wretched doctor let me out." Hyde said.

Kane stands up, facing Hyde. Hyde looks at Kane, smiling.

"Gabriel Kane!" Hyde said. "I'm a big fan of your work. Especially that time when you were in America. Great story."

"Hyde, we don't need any trouble here." Kane said. "Just let Jekyll out and we'll call it a night."

Hyde holds his chin, thinking. He looks down at Kane, who's only staring at him.

"Well?" Kane said.

"Nope!" Hyde mocked.

Hyde backhands Kane into the wall. Kane pulls out his pistols and begins firing at Hyde. He jumps around the room, avoiding the pistol shots. Kane stops firing as he sees Hyde in front of him, standing still.

"Ran out of ammo, Kane?" Hyde said smiling.

Kane runs toward Hyde and punches him. Hyde staggers, but catches Kane's next punch and slams him on the ground. Kane looks and sees Hyde's foot above him. Kane rolls out of the way as Hyde's foot goes into the floor, breaking the wood. Hyde sees that his foot is stuck in the broken wood. He desperately tries to pull it out as Kane attacks him with his rapier and cutlass. While Kane was attacking Hyde, he noticed that his saliva was similar to that of the deceased man and woman he previously saw. Hyde smacks Kane back and pulls his foot out of the wood. Hyde turns and sees Kane on the ground. He runs and jumps, Kane pulls out one pistol and aims it at Hyde. He fires and Hyde falls to the ground.

Kane looks and sees Hyde reverting to Jekyll. Kane turns him over on his back and sees that he shot him in the chest.

"Jekyll, I'm truly sorry." Kane said. "But, it was your doing."

"I shall thank you, Gabriel Kane." Jekyll said. "For now, I'm free."

"Yet, you are." Kane said.

"Though, I was meant to send you a message, if we ever came into contact." Jekyll said.

"Which is?"

"I've been under the control of Count Dracula. He's the reason why my alter ego has been causing havoc."

Dracula? Why tell me now?!"

"Because, if you were to kill me, he would like to see you. In fact, he's been wanting to meet you for a while now."

Kane watches as Jekyll gave up the ghost. He leaves him in the church and exits the building. He gets onto his horse, returning to the priest.

Kane returns to the priest and tells him that Dr. Jekyll is dead. The Priest looks at Kane with a little uncertainty. Kane walks toward a table, covered with a map of certain locations across Europe. Kane looks up and places his finger on one particular location. The Priest walks over and looks at the location.

"That's Transylvania, Gabriel." The Priest said.

"I am aware. Dr. Jekyll said Dracula desires to meet me. I intend on traveling to Transylvania to encounter him. Just to see what he wants."

"I do not know why Dracula would want to see you, Gabriel. Unless, he requires you to do a bidding of his."

"I do a lot of biddings, you know that for sure." Kane said with a smirk.

Kane gathers more equipment and ammo before leaving the church. As Kane walks toward the door, he turns and faces the Priest. The Priest nods as Kane smiles, leaving the church. Outside, Kane rides the horse into the clear, quiet streets, that lead to the mountains.

Kane travels through the deserted streets, he reaches the mountains. According to the map, Transylvania lies just above the mountains. Kane looks up at the dark and foggy mountains, not seeing any source of a trail or lead to Transylvania or Dracula. Kane, instead makes a left turn, entering a small forest. Kane travels through the forest. It's quiet, and foggy. As Kane travels through, he stumbles upon a cemetery. Kane looks at the cemetery, as he looked he spots what appears to be a white dress running through the cemetery. Kane stops his horse and goes to look. He pulls out his pistols, walking slowly into the foggy cemetery.

"Mmm." Kane uttered. "Anybody here? I saw you."

A white mist passes from behind Kane as quick as a light. Kane turns, not seeing anything behind him. He continues walking deeper into the cemetery. He now spots something that looks like the dress he saw, standing behind the tree, covered in shadow. Kane walks to the tree.

"Excuse me." Kane said.

Kane looks and sees a woman, who appears as mist. Her face appears reminiscent of a skull. She looks at him and shrieks loudly. Kane covers his ears, trying to block out the loud and painful scream. She flies by Kane and knocks him down. Kane rolls over and starts firing at the mist, knowing that the pistol has no effect on the apparent ghost. Kane gets back on his feet and notices that there's two more mists flying around the cemetery. He spots one and pulls out his rapier sword.

"Who's first?" Kane said.

One mist flew toward him, screaming in pain. Kane ducks and slices through the mist with his rapier. The mist screams and flies into the air. Kane spots the other two approaching him. He stands still, holding the rapier, preparing to slash them. As he raises the rapier, a bright light appears from behind him, causing the mists to fly off into the distant. The light dims and Kane turns, seeing a woman with long black hair and wearing Victorian attire. Kane looks and places his rapier by his side.

"What are you doing here?" The woman asked.

"I thought I saw someone out here.' Kane said. 'So, I went to look. Who are you?'

"My name is Victoria Gretchen. Descendant of the Gretchen Liege."

"I've heard of that name before. I'm Gabriel Kane. What are you doing out here?"

"I was traveling through the forest, until I heard that shriek. So, I came to see what the problem and the problem was just you."

"I'm not the problem, miss. I'm looking for a way to Transylvania and to Dracula."

"You're looking for Dracula?" Victoria said.

"Do you have any clue where I can reach Transylvania?" Kane asked. "I heard that it's behind these mountains. Is that the case?"

"Transylvania is indeed behind those mountains.' Victoria said. 'But, if that's where you're going, you'll need my assistance."

"I'm sorry, miss. But, I work alone. It's what I do best."

Victoria smiles as Kane looks at her weary.

"Well, now you'll have to deal with a traveling teammate. First, we need to reach the lower town. To the east."

"Why the lower town? What's there that we could use?"

"The villagers know the exact trail to Transylvania. Besides, it's where I live."

Kane and Victoria head off into the darkness toward the lower town.


It is now daylight, cloudy morning as Kane and Victoria arrive at the lower town. Villagers roam the main town area, buying food and supplies. Kane looks around the area.

"I don't see how you could live here." Kane said.

"Why is that?" Victoria said.

"Because you don't seem to fit here. By your appearance, it doesn't seem that you could be living here."

"For one, I grew up here as a child. I was born in London, but my family decided that the city wasn't their type of standards. What about yourself, Kane?"

"Never really knew my blood family. Such is a very long story."

Victoria walks toward an old building, that appears to be housed of elderly villagers. Kane walks behind her, as the villagers look and stare at him. Some appear as if they are afraid of him. Kane follows Victoria through the building.

"These people seem to fear me. I do not know why."

"The people across this land know who you are and what you've done. You might not know this, but, you're famous to them."

"I don't see how. I'm only a monster hunter and ufologist. I don't see how that's being called famous. I would suspect ridicule or distain. Some form of persecution would do nicely."

"Trust me, it's around."

Victoria finds a wooden box in the corner of the building. She walks over and pulls out a key, opening the box. Kane walks toward her and looks into the box. He sees a large amount of ammo and weapons.

"Where did these come from?" Kane said.

"They were my father's. Like yourself, my father was on a quest to find Dracula some time ago. Unfortunately, he didn't succeed in finding him."

"Sorry about that. Well, for now, we can accomplish your father's goal. You and I."

Victoria turned, staring at Kane.

"At first, you wanted to do this alone. Now, you want to do this with me. Someone had a change of heart or something?"

"No." Kane said. "It's just that since your father was on the same journey as I, it would be suiting that you can be involved as well. Achieving your father's goal."

"I see."

They look throughout the box, sounds of screams are heard from the outside. Victoria and Kane run to the front door, leading to the outside. They reach the outside and see villagers running in panic as a swarm of vampires chase them. Killing the ones that can't run as fast.

"Vampires!" Kane said. "They belong to Dracula."

"Who else could own an army of vampires." Victoria said. "Come on!"

Victoria and Kane attack the vampires. Kane fires at them with his pistol, shooting one in its wing, causing it to crash into a house. Victoria pulls out a pistol from her back and shoots one vampire in the head. She fires at the others surrounding both her and Kane. Kane reloads one pistol and a vampire lands in front of him. Kane goes for a punch, the vampire catches his fist and kicks him in the stomach, knocking him into a wall. Victoria looks and fires at the vampire, hitting it in the shoulder. Kane stands up and runs toward the vampire. Kane punches the vampire and pulls out his rapier sword, slicing the vampire in two.

"Good one." Victoria said.

They continue fighting off the remaining vampires. Kane reaches into his trench coat pocket, pulling out a small bottle of water. One vampire spot it and screeches toward the other vampires. They turn and fly off into the sky. Victoria, confused, turns to Kane. Spotting the Holy Water in his hand.

"They fled." Victoria said.

"I noticed. Probably the water.'

"One of their primary weaknesses." Victoria said. "Along with the cross."

"Not exactly. The cross is a dud. Takes a stronger force to eliminate them. Believe me, I've seen it."

Kane looks around, seeing the villagers surrounding both him and Victoria.

"It was them!" A villager yelled. 'They brought that plaque upon us!"

"No!" Victoria yelled. "We did not. You all know for a fact that vampires have always entered this location to feed. This was only one of their outings."

Kane walks toward Victoria. Looking around the area for any signs of the vampires. He also looks at the number of villagers that surround him and Victoria.

"Do you have any idea where those vampires fled?" Kane asked.

"They went east." Victoria said. "If we follow them, they should lead us to Dracula."

"Good."

After gathering the gear out of the box, Victoria and Kane left the lower town, following the trail of blood left from a few fleeing vampires. After hours of tracking, the trail leads them to a small cave. They enter the cave, its dark, damp, and cold. The only sound throughout the cave is the sound of water flowing in the darkness.

"What could possibly live in here?" Victoria said.

"Anything from rodents to dragons." Kane said.

"Dragons?" Victoria said with a stare.

"Yeah, I've ran into a few one time." Kane said.

Kane takes one step forward, he feels something rough under his boot. He stops and looks down as Victoria stops behind him.

"Kane, what is it?" Victoria said.

"This isn't rock I'm standing on. Something else."

Kane looks down and sees a scaly tail. He jumps off and the tail slithers deeper into the cave. Victoria goes to turn back to the entrance. Kane grabs her by the arm, not letting her leave the cave.

"What are you doing?!" Victoria said. "You've seen the size of that tail?!"

"I've faced worse throughout my lifetime. Come on, we need to find out what's at the end of this cave."

They walk further down into the cave. They reach an apparent dead-end, Victoria turns to Kane. He looks around not finding another way around the dead end. He looks behind Victoria and sees the scaly tail. He points to that direction and follows it. Victoria turns and runs behind Kane. Kane runs as he follows to keep track of the tail. He turns from corner to corner, following the tail. Victoria tries to keep up with him.

"Slow down, Kane."

"This tail is leading us somewhere! 'We have to find out where!"

Kane turns one final corner before facing the creature that the tail belonged to. Victoria runs behind him and stops as she sees the huge scaly creature staring at her and Kane. Kane pulls out his rapier, staring at the scaled beast. The creature roars at them with its wings flapping. Kane holds his hat as the wind is so intense.

"What is this beast?!" Victoria screamed.

"It appears to be a Basilisk with wings. Dragon wings at most." Kane said. "I've never believed in these things."

Kane raises his pistol and fires at the beast. The shot had grazed the beast's head, just above the right eye. It shakes its head and rams over into Kane, knocking him down. Victoria raises her sword and starts to stab the creature. It roars in pain as she continues diving the sword into its side.

The beast swipes Victoria across the small area of the cave. Kane jumps onto the beast, trying to reach for its head. The beast shakes Kane off and tries to bite his leg, only for Victoria to run over and cut the tongue of the beast.

"Great work." Kane said.

The beast staggers as blood dripped from its mouth. It rams toward Victoria, exiting the small area of the cave. Kane walks over to her, helping her up. As she gets to her feet, she looks behind Kane, noticing a locked wooden door.

"There's a door." Victoria said.

She runs over to the door. As she notices a chained lock on the handle. Kane pulls out his pistol and shoots the lock off of the door handle. Victoria looks at him as he opens the wooden door. Behind the door is a small tunnel with light at the end. They walk towards the light and as they get closer, they can hear a man talking. They decide to run towards the light. Once they reached the end, they noticed that they were in a castle corridor. Kane looks to his left and turns to his right, he spots a male, wearing nothing but black turn the corner.

"This way." Kane said.

They follow the man in black to his location. Once they found the location, the man was standing in the middle of the room, covered in marble, with a huge window at the front, overlooking the front of the entire castle as the moon shined down upon it.

"It appears you have been looking for me, Gabriel Kane." The man said.

Kane pauses and looks at Victoria, who is speechless.

"Who are you?" Kane said.

The man turns around and stares at Kane with a smile. Victoria's facial expression shows that she knows exactly who the man in black really is.

"It's him.' Victoria said softly.

"Dracula." Kane said with a determined voice.

Kane stares directly toward Dracula. Their eyes locked on one another. Kane's hand slowly reaching for his pistol. Dracula stares deeply through Kane, smirking.

"Reaching for your pistol, Gabriel Kane." Dracula said.

"How do you know me? We've never met."

"I know everything that's needed to know. Besides, I've heard a lot about you. Your days over in the States during their Civil War, you're time against the Shogun's undead and their captive extraterrestrials."

"How do you know this?"

"I also remember you facing those demons with the Finder and taking on the Wolfman. You've been through a lot of trials at such a young age."

"All you need to know is that I've come here to kill you."

Dracula walks toward Kane, slowly. Kane raises up his pistol and aims it directly at Dracula's heart.

"Go on. Shoot me. Shoot me and you would've accomplished what you came for."

Kane holds the pistol, still aiming at Dracula's heart. Victoria looks at Dracula walking toward Kane as she turns to Kane, forcing him to shoot Dracula. Kane is caught in a daze as he doesn't understand how Dracula knows his history.

"GABRIEL!" Dracula yelled. "SHOOT ME! END MY LIFE AS YOU WISHED!"

Kane fires, shooting Dracula in the heart. Dracula stumbles as Kane and Victoria watch. Dracula stands still and rubs the wound. He turns to Kane, laughing. Kane and Victoria start to worry as Dracula was not wounded from the shot.

"What is this? I shot you in the chest!"

"I'm not like your past adversaries, Gabriel. I am beyond what you fully understand!"

Kane pulls out his rapier and starts to slash at Dracula. He dodges every move from Kane. Dracula moves toward the left of Kane, he grabs him by his coat and slams him into the brick wall.

"Highly determined to kill me." Dracula said. "But, you don't fully understand."

Victoria pulls out her sword and stabs Dracula from behind. He stands still, laughing at Victoria. He reaches toward his back, pulling out the sword. Victoria backs up slowly as Dracula turns toward her and tosses her back the sword. She catches it and stares. Dracula bows before her.

"Impressive, my lady. Impressive indeed."

She runs toward Dracula. Delivering kicks and punches at him. He's quickly dodging them. He moves to the right and kicks her in the abdomen, knocking her into the wall behind her. As he walks toward her, behind him, Kane is staggering to get to his feet. Kane reaches into his pocket and pulls out the water. As Dracula walks slowly toward a downed Victoria, Kane lunges at Dracula. Kane opens the bottle and pours all of the water onto Dracula's face. Dracula shakes and twitches on the ground, clawing at his face and body. Victoria gets to her feet and stands on the side of Kane, watching Dracula on the ground. After a quick second, Dracula stops moving and turns his head, looking at Kane and Victoria. He smiles at them and laughs.

"Blessed Water." Dracula said. "Good choice. Too bad it doesn't work."

Kane slowly backs up, looking at Victoria.

"I thought the water would have an effect on him." Victoria uttered.

"It appears that it doesn't. We need to figure out something else."

"Agreed."

Kane runs toward Dracula and slams him into the ground. Kane gets over him and starts to pummel Dracula with punches. Victoria watches on as Kane continues beating Dracula to a pulp. Dracula doesn't even attempt to counter an attack as he only laughs as Kane pummels him.

"Why won't you die?!" Kane yelled.

"I am already dead! I would expect you to have known that before you've come to see me."

Dracula shoves Kane and kicks him into the air and watches as he falls to the ground, grunting. Dracula gets to his feet, walking slowly toward Kane on the ground. Kane reaches for his pistol, but Dracula speeds over and snatches it.

"Your guns won't do you any good. For you have already attempted its use upon me."

Dracula walks toward the windows and looks outside at the full moon rising above the clouds. He turns toward Kane as Victoria runs over to him, helping him up slowly, as he appears to be bleeding from the mouth.

"I believe that we should save this for another time, yes." Dracula said as he opens up the windows.

He looks back again at Kane and Victoria. They notice that he's transforming. Giant leathery wings span out from behind him. His head starts to change shape, as his teeth sharper and his eyes turn red as blood. Dracula has now fully transformed into a giant humanoid bat. He screeches at them and flies out the windows. Kane runs over to the windows, seeing Dracula in the sky, flying off into the distant, trailing the moonlight.

"This isn't over." Kane declared with intention. "This is definitely not over."

# WEREWOLVES AND VAMPIRES

## 1890
# EUROPE

Late October of 1890, sightings of Dracula have risen to an extreme, so extreme that the Venatores have sent Gabriel Kane to follow these sightings to track Dracula down. Kane's ultimate goal is to kill Dracula and vanquish him from the earth, now he has that opportunity in searching for him and his supposedly new castle in the mountains of Europe.


Kane decided to travel through the valleys, where the first sightings surfaced. He spotted old homes and carts but saw nor heard anyone. As his horse slowly walked through the small pairs of homes. The surroundings were silent. Only the whistling of the cold. Kane knew this was uncommon, especially in the location which he moves through. Without notice, a small gang of vampires, dressed in villager clothing bolt out from the bushes around Kane and move to attack him. Kane revealed his rapier and started to slash the vampires with the silver blade. The vampires scurried away from the scene, in fear of the blade. Kane placed the blade into its sheath and continued. Moving further out of the valleys, he hears a sound in the tress nearby.

"More of them." He said, believing them to be the vampires again.

Upon moving closer, his vision went black as he was attacked from behind and dragged away.


Kane awoke from the fall from the trap. He saw Victoria and Tom to his left, all of them tied to chairs with their hands behind their backs. Kane scouted the surroundings, knowing they're inside a cabin. He saw his weapons and gear sitting on a wooden table not too far from himself. Kane pulled himself over toward the table. As he moved, he caught the sound of the cabin door opening and closing. He moved himself back, seeing a young man and woman. They walked in and stared at Kane, the young woman stared at Kane, running to him with a knife in her hand.

"What were you doing over here?!" The young woman yelled.

"Relax." The young man said. "He's not going anywhere. He's tied up."

"Why am I tied up?" Kane asked. "Who are you two?"

"We're what people like you should fear." The young woman said.

"We're called the Night Watchers." The young man said. "We scout the night to stop any monsters or creatures from causing harm to the living."

Kane nodded.

"So, you're telling me you have no idea who I am?" Kane said. "Not an ounce of a clue?"

"It doesn't matter who you or your people are." The young woman said. "What matters is why were the three of you out at this time of night."

Victoria slowly moved as she began to regain consciousness. When she began to have a clear view of the area, she saw the young man and woman and realized she's tied to the chair by her wrists.

"Where am I? Who are you people?"

"Like we told your friend over there, we're the Night Watchers." The young woman said.

"What do you want from us?" Victoria said.

"We want answers, damn it!" The young woman said. "Nothing less than that!"

Tom woke up from the young woman's yelling. She looked to him. He attempted to move as well, but couldn't because of the tied ropes.

"What the devil is this?" Tom asked. "Where am I? Kane? Victoria?"

"I'm going to ask this question again." The young woman said. "Who are you people and what were you doing out this late?"

They heard the front door open and in walked an middle-aged man, wearing a gray hat and coat. The young man and woman turn and move to the side of the cabin as the man walks over to the three. He looked at them and stopped at Kane. Squinting his eyes to get a better look.

"I know you." The man said. "You're Gabriel Kane, the monster hunter and ufologist. Word travels abroad about your achievements and adventures."

"Wait, he is?" The young woman said.

"Indeed." The man said. "Riley, please untie them."

The young man and woman untie Kane, Victoria, and Tom. Kane stands up and goes for his weapons and gear as the man walks over to him.

"It's an honor to meet a legend in our field." The man said.

"Legend?" Kane said. "I'm just doing what needs to be done."

"Sorry about them tying you and your people up." The man said. "They're very strict when it comes to trespassers."

"So, what your name?" Kane said.

"I'm Raymond Rogers." The man said. "The young girl is Riley Hazelwood and the young man is Connor Hartley."

"Sorry about yelling at you." Riley said.

"Don't bother. You were just doing what needed to be done."

Raymond watched Kane set up his gear.

"If you don't mind, Kane, where were you three headed off to?" Raymond asked.

"Looking for Dracula's new castle. Sightings have surfaced and we intend on ending them and Dracula permanently."

"Funny you say such a thing." Raymond said.

"Why is that?" Kane said.

"Because that's who we're hunting down as well." Connor said. "The big baddie himself."

"That so?" Victoria said. "You know of Dracula and his intentions?"

"Of course, ma'am." Raymond said. "We do what must be done. That's the reason why we're out here."

"So, I take it you do it your way and I do this my way." Kane said. "That way, neither of us will get in each other's way."

"The guy is smart for a change." Riley said.

"Why don't we all travel together." Connor said. "The more of us there is, the easier it will be to track down Dracula and get past his army."

"Dracula now has a pack of werewolves at his disposal." Kane said. "By that count lots of people will be easily tracked down by them."

"Not if we're skilled." Riley said. "I'm good with a sword. Some slicing would do us a service out there against his forces."

"I have the bow and arrow to back it up." Connor said. "Quick and quiet is my asset."

Kane looks at them and turns to Raymond.

"What about yourself?' Kane said. "What field are you useful in terms of weapons?"

"I'm one of the greatest gunslingers and occultist that ever lived in Europe." Raymond said. 'I can hold my own and then some. You'll see when we head out there."

Kane nodded.

"Fair enough." Kane said. "Let's all go hunting."

They grab their weapons and gear and leave the cabin. As they walk outside of the cabin, a gray werewolf lurks at them from atop a small hill and runs off into the woods.

The werewolf climbed up massive amounts of hills and reached a castle. One of old construction. Gothic in nature, yet ancient. As it climbed the castle, it reached the top floor and on top stood Dracula. The werewolf paused and stood still in front of Dracula and was intimidated by his presence.

"What do you have for me on this day." Dracula said. "Anything useful to decipher."

He walked over to the werewolf, glaring into its eyes. By doing such, he saw Kane, Victoria, and Tom speaking with the Night Watchers and leaving the cabin.

"It seems Gabriel has more company. It won't matter very long."

Dracula turned to one of his assistants. Staring toward them with his glaring eyes.

"Command the herd to track them down. Make sure they kill them."

He turned back toward the werewolf. Petting it on its head.'

"You're doing a very good service for your lord. Now, go back out there to help the herd track them and bring some backup with you."

The werewolf climbed onto the wall, jumping from the roof as Dracula grinned, over viewing the valley.


Kane and the Watchers walked throughout the woods, not spotting anything that seems to be vampire or werewolf relatable. Keeping their eyes closely to their surroundings. Which were dark and only to be seen with the glimpses of moonlight.

"Haven't ran into anything yet." Connor said.

"Keep your eyes open, young one." Raymond said. "Be at your guard at all times."

From the woods, bolted out a small army of vampires. Snarling with their teeth toward them. They stood together, forming a circle in front of the vampires. Kane held his gun out in front as did the others.

"When they come for us, fire." Kane said. "Make sure to aim for their heads."

"We've done this before." Riley said. "This isn't some new thing for us."

"Show some decency, Riley." Raymond said. "Do as the man said."

The vampires lunged at them, they fired their guns toward the vampires with Riley slicing them with her sword and Connor shooting arrows into their heads and mouths.

"Take this." Connor said, firing an arrow into a vampire's mouth.

Using the techniques they know, they eliminate the vampires and nod toward each other in their small victory. Upon walking away, Kane turned seen three werewolves staring them down from atop a hill in the distance.

"We're not finished yet." Kane said to the group as they gazed toward the three werewolves atop the hill.

"What should we do?" Victoria said.

"If they start running down and lunge, we kill them. But they seem to be of a different mission."

"What do you mean a different mission?" Riley said. "You mean they're not here to kill us?"

"They could if they wanted to. But it appears they're up to something else."

The werewolves continue to stare down at Kane, Victoria, Tom, and the Watchers. As they slowly crawl down the hill toward them, snarling with saliva dripping from their mouths and their fowl stench inching closer, Raymond turned to Kane.

"So, what do we do now?!" Raymond said.

"We fight if they run down." Kane said. "Kill them just as we did with those vampires."

The werewolves seem to prepare themselves for the attack, but immediately pause and run away, whining, as if they were startled. Catching Kane and the group off their guard, they look around for the werewolves and cannot find them anywhere.

"Where did they go?" Riley said.

"They ran off." Kane said. "But, why?"

Stomping sounds are heard coming from behind Kane and the group. To which they turn around to see and find themselves face to face with hybrid creatures. Drooling and snarling at them.

"The hell are those?!" Connor said.

"I know what they are." Kane said. "They're called the Beast Folk. Human and animal hybrid creations."

"Created by whom?" Victoria said.

"I know a guy."

The Beast Folk roar as they run toward Kane and the group, who are already prepared for the fight ahead.

Meanwhile, at the castle, Carmilla sits with Dracula inside of his main room, gazing out through the windows, overseeing the mountains with the moon above them. She slowly places her arm across Dracula's shoulders and kisses him on his cheek. He chuckled and shook his head.

"No need to try and seduce me, Carmilla. You know that I am already dead and not alive. Also, I am aware that you have no interest in the pleasures of men."

"With time, many things can change."

"Not things such as we have spoken. It appears you want to say something to me."

"I have a proposition for you, if you would like to hear it."

"I am listening."

"I thought since you're planning on ruling this world and I am here to witness it take full circle. How about we both rule the world? A dual ruler-ship?"

"Dual ruler-ship?" Dracula said. "You must be joking with me."

"I am not joking with you, Lord Dracula. I am being completely honest with you on this one."

"Very well, Carmilla. I will be completely honest with you when I say no."

"No?"

"That's right. No. This world is only meant to be ruled by one individual and that individual will be me."

Dracula turned and walked away from the windows. Tossing Carmilla's arm from his shoulders. She gazed at him with anger, but pressed it down as she wanted to see the outcome of the long-term planning.

"Carmilla, focus on your part and everything will go as planned."

In the woods near the mountains and hills, Kane and the group battle it out with the Beast Folk. Many have already been killed by the group and only two of them stand remaining. Kane tackles one and shoots it in the head, while Victoria and Raymond deal with the other Beast.

"Just kill the thing!" Kane said.

Victoria raised up her sword and chopped the head of the Beast completely off its body. Its head rolled across the dirt and the surroundings were silent.

"What person would create such abominations?" Raymond said.

"Doctor Moreau." Kane said. "He's working with Dracula."

They continued to walk through the woods, nearing the mountains in the horizon. Upon coming close to the mountains, they find themselves near a large body of water and atop the water laid an island. With a large structure upon it. Kane looked up and pointed toward the island.

"What is that up there?" Kane said.

The group looked up toward the island. Uncertain of what to make if it. Victoria looked and could recognize the structure. She turned to Kane, while looking at the large and tall structure.

"Kane, it's a castle."

"A castle?" Thomas said. "Who's castle?"

"I may have an idea as to who resides on in that castle."

"What do you mean by that?"

"That would explain why those Beast Folk came at us so easily. We were near their place of creation. That island is the Island of Moreau.


Kane and his crew reach the island. An island that's known for Doctor Moreau's creations. They walk toward the large building.

"Is this where Moreau's Beast-Folk were created?" Riley said.

"Some." Kane said. "This island appears to be the place for the other work he's had a hand in occupying."

Kane bolted through the front entrance, entering the main laboratory. Only finding old remains of surgeon tables and doctoral tools, Kane gazed the area continually, spotting two doors, both lead deeper into the building.

"He's not here?" Victoria asked.

"Doesn't appear to be." Kane replied. "However, those two doors could give us the answers we need."

"So, we'll have to split up." Riley said. "Easy tracking."

"As it may be." Raymond said.

"Very well." Kane replied. "Myself, Raymond, and Tom will check the left door. Victoria, you, Riley, and Connor will search the right door."

"And what if we don't find anything?" Conner asked.

"We all return to this spot. We'll give out details if we find any then."

The groups split and went there separate ways. Behind the left door waited a long hallway. Kane nodded as they entered. On the right, waited another hallway, yet, with doors on both sides. Unsure if they were entrances to other labs, restrooms, bedrooms, or anything else of such nature. Victoria shook her head as they entered. Riley kept his right hand on the handle of her sword. Connor had his bow ready with an arrow already in place.

Kane, Raymond, and Tom continued moving stealthy down the left hallway. Not seeing any doors or any exit points in their reach. Tom was frightened of what could happen. Raymond had his revolvers in hand, Kane was prepared for a fight. Whether it were against a vampire, werewolf, or another beast folk.

"I must ask." Tom said, gazing around. "What happens if we don't find Doctor Moreau?"

"What do you mean?" Kane asked.

"Well, if he's not here, then, where will he be?"

"He could be somewhere roaming the area for all we know." Raymond said. "I'm positive he wouldn't go too far from this place."

"Maybe he would." Kane said.

"Why is that?" Tom asked.

"He's working with Dracula. If he needed a quick place to hide or to continue his work in secrecy, Dracula's castle is the perfect hiding spot. The perfect place to create monsters of his own making."

"Yes." Raymond added. "And, if he were to create monsters under Dracula's rule, those beasts could very well form Dracula's new army."

"An army of vampires, werewolves, and beast folk?" Tom said. "This isn't going very well is it."

"It's certainly not."


Meanwhile, on the right side, Victoria, Riley, and Connor search the rooms within the hallway. Only finding them to be closet spaces for surgery tools, some restrooms, and one storage room.

"I must ask, why are the two of you with the older man?"

"Because he saved us." Riley said.

"Saved you? From what?"

"A werewolf attack." Connor said. "Our parents were ambushed by werewolves. Raymond appeared and saved us.'

"You're brother and sister?"

"No." Riley said. "We lived in the same village. The werewolf had appeared and slaughtered most of the villagers. My family was killed first before Connor's. Raymond saved us and believed we needed to be watched over. So, he took us in as one of his own."

"And the monster hunting?"

"Once we were older, Raymond told us of his profession. Hunting monsters. That explained why he appeared in the village during the attack. We've never seen him before that. So, in order to protect us, he trained us. I learned how to wield a sword. Connor grew in the skill of archery."

"I see."

"After our training, we went out with Raymond on hunts." Connor said. "Saving lives and killing monsters. We were given the name 'The Night Watchers' because of our efforts."

Victoria nodded.

"Do either of you miss the childhood days or do you wish you didn't have to live this life?"

"I've grown into this." Riley said. "I'm better off protecting others from what I suffered."

"And I loved the thrill of the hunt." Connor smirked. "Vampires, werewolves, gargoyles, anything that's a challenge makes this all worthwhile."

While walking on the checkered floors, Connor spotted another door in front of them. Directly in place, a two-door entrance to another room.

"Maybe, something's in there." Connor said.

"As always." Riley added. "We'll have to check it out."

"Agreed." Victoria replied.

Opening the double-doors, they find themselves in a large room. Not as large as the front laboratory. But, within they see tables. Long tables lined up parallel to each other. Victoria looked around and knew what the room was.

"This place is a dining hall."

"A dining hall?" Connor said. "In a dump like this."

"I'm guessing this was a place for scientists before they left it." Riley said.

"It seems so."

Checking out the beaten-down hall, a stumbling sound of glass shattered behind them. They turned with quick pace as the double-doors shut. Connor raised up the bow, Riley twirled the sword, Victoria held his blade. Each was ready for the fight. Connor looked around, not seeing anything in the darkness. Only the moon was the light source.

"Do you hear that?" Riley asked.

They listened and what they could hear were footsteps. Each step inching closer. They manage to look and standing before them was one of the beast folk, standing approximately seven-feet in height, and its skin torn and hairy, upper body was of a man. The lower was of a goat... A Satyr-Man. Victoria jolted with the blade in place, Riley held the sword still, Connor fired an arrow. The arrow pierced the Satyr-Man in the arm. It pulled the arrow from its body and shrieked. Lunging toward them. Connor moved from its path and fired another arrow while Riley ran up toward the creature, slashing it with her sword. Victoria wielded her blade and attacked the creature from behind, Riley took the front, and Connor circled the Satyr-Man. Each one delivering attacks on the creature. The Satyr-Man swiped its arm toward Riley, who ducked down and slashed the ankles of the creature. The beast folk fell to one knee, where Victoria jumped on its back, stabbing it in many places. Connor ran up and fired two arrows into the eyes of the creature. The Satyr-Man knocked Victoria from its back and ran forward, impaling itself into Riley's sword. The creature still attempted to grab Riley and eventually died due to the sword impaled through its heart and the amount of blood that had fallen.

"See." Connor said. "That was a challenge."

"What kind of creature was that?" Riley asked.

"One of Moreau's experiments." Victoria replied. "Come on, we need to tell the others."


Upon them returning to the lab, they found them already waiting on them. Now regrouped, they each told one another of their findings. Kane, Raymond, and Tom found nothing. No sign of Moreau. Victoria told Kane of their encounter with the Satyr-Man and their lack of finding Moreau. Kane took all the information in and quickly knew where the doctor was located.

"We need to go to Dracula's castle. They're all there."

"I must ask." Connor said. "What if they're waiting on us to come?"

"Then, it makes this task very easy."

The following day, word had spread to the neighboring lands of strange activities of an sudden arrival of a strange and dark castle atop Mount Elbrus.

Within the castle, Dracula waited patiently, staring out of the large open window. Carmilla approached him from behind, gazing out toward the small village and snowy range of the mountain.

"Have you done what you've offered to do?" Dracula asked.

"I have. The armies are prepared and ready for your command."

Dracula nodded.

"Excellent. Because we have guests in a matter of time."

"Guests?" Carmilla questioned. "You speak of the hunter and his allies?"

"Who else do I speak of. I'm positive they visited the Doctor's island and found not him. Therefore, Gabriel Kane knows he's here with us and they're coming."

"Perhaps I can make a distraction. A diversion of sorts. Weaken them for you."

Dracula turned to Carmilla and agreed. She exited the room and right after came Moreau. Hesitant to speak with Dracula. But, it would be necessary if he did.

"You've heard the news haven't you?" Dracula asked.

"I am aware the hunters invaded my island and entered my laboratory. The signals have went off."

"And you are aware hey are headed here. To find us all and eliminate us."

"I figured such a thing would happen. It explains the vampire and werewolf armies outside at the gates.

"What of your beast folk?"

"What of them, my lord?"

"Are they ready for the fight to come?"

"Oh, yes." Moreau grinned. "They are ready."

"Then, make way."

Moreau bowed and left Dracula to himself, who continued to look outside. Patiently awaiting the arrival of Kane.


After some mere hours of travel, Kane and the group stood at the entrance to the small town. There, the townspeople rushed toward him, telling him of the strange castle that stood on Mount Elbrus. Victoria turned to Kane, while gazing up at the mountain in the distance, they could see the castle for themselves.

"He's there." Kane said. "He's in there right now. Looking down at us."

"How can you be sure he's looking at us?" Riley asked.

"I just know."

Just as Kane said, Dracula was indeed looking down toward them. Still in the same place as he was hours before. Only, this time, he felt a jolt go through his body. Dracula shrugged the pain away.

"He's here. He's down there."

Kane and the group prepared to make way toward the mountain. Knowing that the possibility of reaching it during sunup is a slight chance. More so, they estimate their arrival at the gate of the castle directly at nightfall, which will cause more trouble for them in the form of vampires and werewolves. Not to mention Moreau's beast folk.

"How do we proceed?" Tom wondered. "Do we just walk in or do we move quietly?"

"We'll manage." Kane said. "It's going to take all of us to enter the castle. Just leave Dracula to me."

"Understood." Tom replied.

"And what of the vampires, werewolves, and those other things?" Connor asked. "We'll handle them I suppose."

"We must." Raymond said. "For we can only wonder what else dwells in such a dark place."

"Very well." Kane said. "Let's get moving."


After some travel, they arrived at the base of Elbrus, looking up at the dark and gothic structure that was the castle. Kane was ready. He blood was pumping, ready to face Dracula. Victoria could sense Kane's anger searing.

"I would keep that inside until you have the opportune moment."

"I agree."

Tom looked up toward the sky and noticed something strange to himself. He pointed, giving signal to the others.

"What is that?" He asked.

Coming down from the sky above hem was Carmilla and six other vampires. Screeching loudly as they made landfall. Carmilla stood in front of them, facing the group. Her smile was beautiful and sinister. Kane pulled out his rapier as did the others.

"Who is she?" Riley asked.

"I am Carmilla, my dear. And you look so beautiful."

"I'm not taking that compliment."

"No bother. Soon, I'll be taking all of you."

"Enough." Kane said. "Where's your boss?"

"My boss?! Gabriel, if you only knew. This is the both of us combined. Our union will shake the foundations of this world and build a new one. One of monsters."

"There's too many humans to make that a possibility." Victoria said.

"Try it when they refuse to fight for themselves."

"We'll fight for them." Connor said.

Carmilla chuckled.

"How kind of you. Take them!"

The vampires went in for the attack. Swiping their clawed hands and talons across the air above them. Kane raised his rapier and slash one's leg. Victoria and Riley managed to bring down two more. Leaving the other three to Tom, Raymond, and Connor. Connor fired several arrows into one, leading it to crash into the snow. Raymond took out his revolvers and shot one in the head.

"This is a trick." Raymond said.

Tom threw a knife toward the last one, but missed.

"Oh dear." Tom uttered.

The vampire rushed toward him and as it inched closer, Kane jumped in between them, stabbing the creature before it could slash Tom's neck.

The vampires were defeated. Carmilla applauded them and flew away.

"After her!" Kane yelled.

They chased Carmilla toward the castle. Moving closer and closer. As they were almost near the entrance. Several of Moreau's beast folk appeared. Halting their progress. Raymond, Riley, and Connor stood against them. Their weapons ready.

"Go!" Raymond yelled to Kane. "We'll hold them off!"

Kane nodded with respect as he, Victoria, and Tom went off to the castle gate. Behind them, they could hear the gunfire, arrows flying, and a sword slashing.

"I hope they make it." Tom said.

"They can take care of themselves." Kane added. "They'll be fine."

Right when they entered the castle, Carmilla flew up and standing before them was Moreau, twirling his hands.

"I am delighted you've come."

"Where's Dracula?" Kane asked.

"He's here. But, you'll only get to him if you can kill my most prized creation."

Walking into the open room was a tall figure. It appeared humanoid, yet, it was hairy and with it came the smell of blood and water.

"The hell is that?" Tom said.

"It is what I call a Vamp-Wolf!" Moreau yelled. "And, it is not alone."

Behind the creature came three werewolves. One grey, another black, and the last one brown. Moreau ran out of the room in a hurry. Kane was agitated to the point where it was everything or nothing. He went for the Vamp-Wolf with his rapier, swiping its chest and legs. The creature backhanded Kane and Victoria went in for the attack herself. Tom was chased around by the werewolves, leading to Kane killing one and standing before the other two. Victoria kicked the beast and the creature grabbed her, throwing her against Kane. During the fight, Dracula entered the room, hoping to gain a closer look and Kane turned to see him.

"Gabriel Kane." Dracula said. "We meet again."

"For the last time." Kane replied.

"Then come. Come and end my life as you desire."

Kane went for Dracula and was snatched by Carmilla from the air and tossed into the wall. Tom saw Dracula walking in the midst of the battles, he reached into his pocket, revealing a small dagger made of silver. Kane stood up, shaking himself. Victoria managed to kill a werewolf while dodging the claws of the Vamp-Wolf. Tom moved quietly behind Dracula, raising the dagger and as it came down, Carmilla grabbed his arm.

"No, my dear. That is not going to happen."

Tom dropped the dagger, Kane saw it fall and it gave him a opening. Possibly. Carmilla held Tom up off the ground, ripping his cloak to reveal his neck. She could feel the blood pulsing through him and it moisturized her. She opened her mouth, unveiling the sharp fangs.

"I need some help over here!" Tom yelled in panic.

Kane grabbed the dagger and Carmilla went for the bite. However, Tom had another blade and pierced it in the heart of Carmilla. She paused with a shocking jolt. Her eyes turned from black to white. The fangs reverted. She dropped Tom and fell to the ground. Dracula watched on. He nodded.

"Impressive from a friar of such low nature."

Kane rushed toward the Vamp-Wolf, stabbing it with the dagger. Victoria jumped up and beheaded the creature. Its body fell as the one werewolf remained. Lunging toward Victoria, only to be shot by Kane's revolver. The room was paused. Dracula clapped his hands in their victory.

"You three are very skilled in the art of the kill. How can you manage such a foe as myself? I can only reveal in battle and in your deaths."

Raymond, Riley, and Connor entered the room, seeing Kane and Dracula facing off. Connor fired an arrow toward the vampire lord. Dracula caught the arrow with ease, breaking it into small shards of wood.

"You're not fit for this kind of challenge, boy."

"This is between you and me." Kane said. "Just us."

"Indeed. But, by the way you look, you're tired. Beaten. I don't want to kill you at your lowest. I want you at your best."

"What are you saying?"

"I will come to you when you are in your best shape. Then, we will battle."

"NO!" Kane went for a shot and Dracula was gone. "Dammit!"


After a bit of calming down, they returned to the small town. Connor looked up at the mountain and noticed the castle was gone. As if it had never been there. Kane knew Dracula moved it. He and Raymond shook hands.

"Are you sure you don't need us to help you in this endeavor?" Raymond asked.

"I'll find him." Kane replied. "It's fate."

Raymond nodded.

"May you kill him for the best."

The Night Watchers left. Tom approached Kane as did Victoria.

"I have to ask, besides finding Dracula, what is next?"

"Finding Dracula." Kane said. "That is all that's next."

# THE SEARCH FOR DR. FRANKENSTEIN

## 1891
# BISMARCK GERMANY

Gabriel Kane heads toward Germany after being contacted by The Knights of The Holy Order to investigate the missing Dr. Victor Frankenstein. Currently, the year is 1891 and Kane has had many encounters that would appear strange to the normal society. As Kane enters Germany on his black horse, he notices the location's areas are covered with pictures of Dr. Frankenstein, all have the word "missing" above his headshot photo.

Kane's first location to investigate is the University of Ingolstadt, the museum that Dr. Frankenstein attended during his early years of studying. Kane always heard rumors that Frankenstein was high on creating life, though it seems that he never succeeded in accomplishing it. Kane enters the university, noticing many physicists walking throughout the campus. He heads toward the front office.

"Excuse me." Kane said to the lady at the front desk. "I'm here to discuss the missing doctor. Dr. Victor Frankenstein."

"Oh, sir.' The lady said. 'We haven't seen or spoken to him in months.'

"Is there a trail that I can follow.' Kane asked. 'Did he mention anywhere he was headed?"

"Last we heard; he was living in the mountains."

"Thank you." Kane said as he left the university.

Kane now travels to the mountains, searching for the missing doctor. As he travels through the crowded forest, heading down the trail, he spots a cabin above him, towards the front of the mountains. Kane commands his black horse to run faster, moving quicker to get a closer look at the cabin. Once, he has a better view, he sees that it's a large cabin, with smoke coming from a pipe in the roof, meaning something's inside. Kane gets off his horse and walks up the pathway heading into the mountains, right at the cabin.

By nightfall, Kane reaches the top of the mountains. He walks slowly toward the large cabin. He stands by the wall, taking a look into the window. He sees nothing inside, but a lab table and some equipment. As he looks deeper into the window, he notices someone walking around. He quickly moves from the window and heads toward the front door. Kane stands by the door, with one hand on the doorknob, the other hand at his side, holding his revolver.

He quickly opens the door to the cabin and walks in. As he enters quietly, the door squeaks as it closes itself. He turns and sees no one behind him. He walks around the cabin, seeing dozens of jars containing human remains and surgeon equipment and tools.

"What was he doing in here?"

Kane continued searching the cabin and its surroundings. As he walks toward the operating table, he hears footsteps from behind. Kane quickly turns and aims his revolver at Dr. Frankenstein.

"Dr. Frankenstein." Kane said. "Where have you been? You've been declared missing by the country of Germany."

"My good sir, I've been here the entire time.' Victor said. 'You look familiar. You're Gabriel Kane, the monster hunter and ufologist.'

"I am. I've been sent by the Symbolum Venatores to find you."

"The Knights?" Victor asked. 'What would they want with me."

"They believe that your grave robberies and goal to create life is turning a little chaotic. They want to stop what you're doing."

Victor stared at Kane as he walked over to his wooden desk, surrounded with jars and paper.

"I cannot stop Mr. Kane." Victor said. "This is my life's work. I do not have anything else to live for."

"You can start a new life. A new journey."

"No. There's no possible way I'm leaving this life and moving on like the rest of you. Besides, my work has already been completed."

Kane pauses.

"What work?"

"The ability to prove that God is not the only one who can create life." Victor said. 'I've accomplished it."

"How do you know you're telling the truth and not some false lie?' Kane asked.

Victor walked over into another room and opened the doors. Kane walked behind Victor as he saw someone sitting down in a chair in the distance.

"Who is that man, Victor?"

Victor commands the man in the chair to stand up and face him as well as Kane. The man stood on his feet; his height was around eight to nine feet in length. He had long black hair that reached his shoulders, he was wearing nothing but torn cloth and what appeared to be a ripped cloak. The man looked up at Victor and pointed at Kane.

"He is my creation." Victor said. "The Adam of my labors."

"A modern Prometheus."

The man walked over to Kane, looking down at him. Kane nods with his hat as the man only growls. Victor pushes the man back away from Kane. Kane only stares at the man, looking at his greenish-grey skin, with knots and bolts in his body.

"You created a creature, Victor." Kane said. "You must get rid of it, immediately."

"Never, Mr. Kane."

Victor turned to the man, whispering something in his ear. Kane only looks on as the man turns his focus on Kane. The man runs over to Kane, knocking him through the cabin wall. Kane rolls onto the ground, reaching for his revolver, seeing the man walk out of the cabin and into the dawning sunlight. The man roars as Kane only stares.

"This is going to be very difficult."

Kane gets to his feet and fires a shot at the creature's leg. The creature stumbles and looks at its leg. It turns to Victor, who commands him to get rid of Kane. The creature runs over to Kane, knocking him into the mountain walls. Victor walks outside and stares at his creation. As it pummels onto Kane. Kane takes out a knife from his coat and swipes at the monster's arm. The monster backs up, holding its arm in pain. Groaning at its arm, it looks at Kane and rams him into the mountain wall. As Kane tries to get to his feet, Victor walks outside as he holds his hands behind his back, watching his monster attack Kane.

"What are you doing, Victor?!"

"Just standing by while my creation destroys you for trespassing." Victor said.

"Trespassing? I was sent here to look for you."

"You see that I'm doing just fine here. Now, just lay there and die."

The monster grabs Kane by his coat and throws him toward the cabin, laying right in front of Victor. Kane looks up and lunges at Victor. Now holding a pistol at Victor's head, the monster stops moving and stares at Victor.

"Tell your monster to step back." Kane said to Victor.

"Stand down, my creation."

The monster steps back as Kane shoves Victor toward it. Kane continues to hold the pistol at Victor and watches closely at the monster.

Now, you will come with me, Victor." Kane said. "That isn't a question."

"I've already said, I'm not going with you."

Kane points and shoots at the monster's leg with his pistol. The monster groans and falls to one knee while holding the injured leg. Victor screams at Kane not to kill his creation. Kane turns to Victor, demanding that he come along with him. As Victor continues to decline, Kane fires another shot at the monster, hitting him in the other leg. Victor goes down to his knees and surrenders to Kane.

"Enough!" Victor yelled. "I'll go along with you. Just please don't kill my creation."

"Fair enough."

Kane placed the pistol back into its holster and takes Victor back to his horse. Kane walks back and grabs his hat off the ground, which fell off during the fight. As Kane prepares to leave, Victor notices his monster staring at him. Victor tells the monster to go back into the cabin and that he'll be safe. The monster nods and enters the cabin. Kane looks ahead and rides off on his horse with Victor in tow.


Back at the Venatores base, Kane brings in Victor to the Order. The Order stare at Victor intensely. One knight walks up to Victor and places his hand on Victor's shoulder.

"It is a proud privilege to see you in our presence, Dr. Frankenstein." the hunter said.

"Why am I here to start with?" Victor said. "What do you want with me?"

"Your unparalleled talent, of course." A hunter said. "We know about your creation, the monster."

Why bring up my precious creation?' Victor said.

Because you have proven that God isn't the only one who can create life." The hunter said. "Which is why we would like you to join us in protecting this plane."

"Protect it from what?"

"I wouldn't expect you to know all the information, doctor. But, you live in a world where evil presents itself in pure form. No hiding, no disguises."

Kane stands up from against the wall, presenting himself in front of the Order.

"What they want is you to work for them and your monster. I'm sure they would like to use him on quests."

Victor looks dazed.

"My creation is not a weapon to be used upon. It is a living being with emotions."

"A living abomination of deceased people, doctor. Sure, it can be used as a weapon."

Victor shakes his hand in disagreement.

"I will never let my creation be used for such purposes.' Victor said.

"It seems that you do not have a choice."

The hunter waves his hand towards the door and as it opens, Victor sees his creation in a cage being rolled into the room. Kane looks and begins to reach for his pistol. The Knight notices him and raises his hand toward him.

"That won't be necessary, Gabriel. We have it under control."

"Are you sure about that?' Kane asked.

The cage is shaking as the monster roars at the Order. Victor walks over towards it, trying to calm it down. He does very little as Kane walks across to the other side of the room, hand still on his pistol.

"If I may ask, what's the main purpose of this monster being here?"

"The same purpose we just told Dr. Frankenstein here. His great creation can be used to protect the world from the evil that lurks."

"Thought that's what I was for." Kane said.

"You are. We just feel it's more suitable to have others to do the work for us as well.'

"Don't hurt my creation!" Victor yelled.

"We're not going to, doctor.' The Knight said. 'You have nothing to worry about here.'

Victor looks around and turns his attention towards the Order.

"I'll help you on your quests.' Victor said. 'As long as my creation isn't harmed in any means.'

"Fair enough." The Knight said. "Welcome, Dr. Victor Frankenstein to the Order.'

The Knight walks over and shakes Victor's hand.

"You're doing a great service for your world and its people."

Kane walks around as the Order turns to him. He realizes it and looks back.

"Kane, you've always done what was right and you have succeeded once again." The hunter said. "We thank you for helping us."

"No problem. It's what I'm here for. So, what's the next quest?"

The hunter smiles and hands Kane a piece of paper, covered with an encryption. Kane reads it and looks at the Knight, smiling.

"I'm on it."

Once outside, Kane gets onto his horse and rides off, heading on his next journey.

# THE INVISIBLE MAN

## 1898
# THE LATE ENLIGHTENMENT

In the mid-winter season of 1898, Dr. Kemp, a fellow British scientist has met with the Symbolum Venatores. He travels all the way to enter their headquarters. As he walks through their temple, seeing many artifacts and paintings from centuries past, he enters their main conference room. As he sits down inside the room, he tells them of many cases being sought out in England by a man who cannot be seen with the naked eye. Once he finishes speaking, the Order declares they will investigate the case, thus contacting Kane.

Kane arrived, entering the conference room, Kemp is nowhere in sight, since he left and returned home.

"You know why you're here, Gabriel." The lead hunter said.

"Another case I suppose. What is it this time?"

"We need you to go to an English village in West Sussex, England to find a man who cannot be seen with the naked eye."

Kane pauses.

"Wait, you're speaking of the cases that have been raising across England." Kane said.

"Of course. We need you to head over there to stop them. Only God knows what more could happen if its not stopped."

"Where's the doctor? Doctor Kemp?"

"He has returned home. You shouldn't have to speak with him. We've already done that part."

"I would like to speak with him myself. Just for my own sake at least."

"If that's what you would like to do, go ahead. You may leave."

Kane nods as he walks out of the room.


Kane leaves the headquarters and heads for Port Burdock. Within a week, Kane enters Port Burdock and looks through the town for Dr. Kemp's location. Traveling through, he spots a house with the name "Kemp" on the side of the door. Kane mounts off his horse and walks toward the front door. He knocks as he hears someone walking towards.

"Who's there?" Kemp asked.

"I am Gabriel Kane. I was sent by the Venatores to speak with you about the man who can't be seen."

Kemp opens the door, smiling.

"Oh, please come on inside, sir."

Kane enters the home as Kemp closes the door. Inside the house is warm, due to the fireplace being set. Kemp allows Kane to sit in the chair facing the fireplace, Kemp sits beside him.

"I was wondering what you knew about this man?"

"His name is Griffin." Kemp said. "I worked with him on finding a way out of his troubles."

"What kind of troubles, if I may ask?"

"He discovered a way to turn objects or life forms invisible. He Didn't have much to do tests on, so he did it onto himself. Thus, becoming the man who cannot be seen."

"How are you sure that its him who's doing these attacks?"

"The reports suggest that the culprit of this cases cannot be seen. The witnesses who were at the site speak of the victims dying in the hands of an invisible force."

"Do you know where I could find him?"

"I have no idea where he could be. He burned his house and all that could lead to him."

"No evidence." Kane said. "Smart of him."

"I'm sure you'll find him, sir. He'll turn up soon enough."

While Kane and Kemp drink their coffee, they hear screams coming from outside the home. Kane gets up and opens the door, seeing a man on a horse ride through. Kane walks over and stops the man.

"What's the problem?" Kane asked.

"There's a incident in Iping." The man said. "The police are shooting at something we can't see."

"It has to be him." Kemp proclaimed.

"An Invisible Man it must be."

Kane gets onto his horse and looks back at Kemp.

"Where are you going, Mr. Kane?"

"I'm going to do what I was sent for."

Kane nods his hat at Kemp and rides off, heading for Iping.


In the streets of Iping, police are shooting at a force they cannot see. One officer walked over to the leading officer.

"What are we shooting at, sir?" The officer asked.

"The man who cannot be seen." The leading officer said.

"How do you know he's still there?"

"Enough with the questions and keep firing at that spot!"

As the officers continue to fire at the spot, the citizens run throughout the town in horror, most of them are leaving through the town as Kane enters. He mounts his horse and runs over to the officers.

"It's him." Kane said.

Kane pulls out his pistol and fires at the location. After he fires, the officers turn to him and he continues to look ahead, spotting the dirt on the ground to bounce up as he someone is running through. Kane shoves the officers out of the way as he chases the Invisible Man.

He follows the trail of dirt that's been shoved around and later finds footprints. He tracks the prints down a few streets and finally into an alleyway. Kane slowly reaches for his pistol as he follows the track, through the other end of the alley, he sees civilians running all over the place, but Kane spots a man leaning against the wall, wearing a brown trench coat and a hat.

Kane looks again and notices that the man has no legs nor a head. The man turned toward him and Kane fired his pistol. The Invisible Man runs down the other street as Kane follows him. When Kane reaches closer to him, The Invisible Man stops and turns toward Kane.

"I suggest you leave me alone."

"I will not." Kane said. "You're coming back to the Venatores with me."

"I think not."

Kane jerks the Man's left arm. The Invisible Man turns.

"If that's the way you want this to go."

The Invisible Man punches Kane, knocking him back as he continues to run off. Kane shakes his head and looks around, spotting the tail end of the trench coat turning right. Kane runs and continues to chase him. As Kane catches up to him, he pulls out his pistol and fires, hitting the Invisible Man in the right leg. The Invisible Man is now limping at he tries to outrun Kane.

As Kane gets closer, The Invisible Man enters a large crowd of people trying to find their way through other areas of the city. Kane rams through the crowd, looking for The Invisible Man. Once through the crowd, Kane looks down and sees the hat and coat that the Invisible Man was wearing with smears of blood on them. Kane uses his blade to cut a cloth off the coat and places it inside his coat pocket. He looks around the snowy areas of the town for other footprints, he spots none.

"Damn it."


Kane returns to Port Burdock to speak with Kemp. As He arrives at Kemp's home and enters, he sits down.

"What happened in Iping?" Kemp wondered.

"I found him. Though, I lost him.'"

"Oh dear."

Kane reaches into his coat pocket and pulls out the cloth from the Invisible Man's coat and hands it over to Kemp.

"It's his blood on the cloth."

Kemp grabs his glasses and observes the cloth. Smiling.

"How did you get this?"

"I shot him in his right leg."

"Excellent work you've done here. I will examine this as soon as possible."

"I thank you for that. I should be leaving now. Most High only knows what I have next on my list."

"Good to see you again, Mr. Kane."

"Always a pleasure."


Kane leaves Port Burdock, returning to the Venatores. The next week, sightings in western Europe have been on the rise of a mysterious Invisible Man causing harm to the villages.

# THE PHANTOM OF THE OPERA
## 1910
# BELLE EPOQUE

In the late winter of January 1910, Gabriel Kane travels to Paris, France to uncover the mystery behind the apparent Opera-Ghost. It is said that the Opera-Ghost appears as a man, wearing opera clothing and a white mask. The Secret Society have told Kane that the Opera-Ghost is always sighted inside the famous Paris Opera House known as *Palais Garnier*. When Kane arrived in Paris, he notices everyone around the downtown area and throughout are wearing the similar white mask that the Opera-Ghost wears. According to the citizens, the mask is known as the Phantom Mask, referring to its appearance and color.

Kane enters a church that's not far away from the Opera House. Inside the church, he is greeted by a young man, short, with brown hair. He's a friar known only as Tom.

"You must be the Gabriel Kane? The Gabriel Kane known across the lands."

"Indeed, I am." Kane said. "You're Tom. The Knights speak heavily of you."

"The Symbolum Venatores?" "They don't even know I exist, yet I work for them."

"They know you exist." Kane said. "You're just not in their high rankings is all."

"Maybe if I could team with you and others, I could be in their sights."

"Me entering this church and meeting you means the Knights have an eye on you. They wouldn't send me here otherwise. Definitely not for a friar of any sort of the imagination."

Kane pulled out a note and handed it to Tom. He put on his glasses and read the note before glancing up at Kane with a blank stare. He held the note above his shoulders.

"You're telling me that the Knights want me to assist you in investigating the Opera-Ghost?"

"Yes. Didn't you just mention that if you could align yourself with me or any of the others, you would be in their sights."

"But that was just me talking out of my ass. I didn't think that it would happen. Not until I became a monk."

Kane takes the note back from Tom and placed it inside his leather coat pocket. Tom only stared as Kane looked at him and glanced toward the church doors.

"We need to go immediately."

"Why immediately? Why not tomorrow?"

"Because tomorrow, the Opera-Ghost could be gone and lost in my sights."

Kane and Tom head toward the opera house, they notice posters and banners covering the exterior of the house as well as other buildings throughout Paris, which represent the Opera-Ghost himself. Tom is terrified by the number of banners that are surrounding Paris for the Opera-Ghost. As more people are seen wearing the ghost masks, they finally arrive at the opera house, where they meet, Viscount Raoul, Vicomte de Chagny.

"Ah! The legendary Gabriel Kane has arrived in Paris." Raoul said. "What a pleasure it is to see you here in Paris."

"The pleasure is all mine." Kane said. "It's been a while since I've stepped foot in Italy."

"It's good to have you here in our presence. I'm sure you're not in the mindset to take a small break so we could have a conversation."

"I'm set for a conversation."

Raoul walks Kane and Tom through the house, seeing many banners and posters that speak of the Opera-Ghost. To the people walking around inside the house, it's just an ordinary trick played by well performed actors. Raoul enters an office room where Kane and Tom follow. They sit in the chairs as Raoul closed the door. He sits by the wooden desk facing Kane.

"So, what was this conversation that you wanted to speak to me about?"

"It concerns the Opera-Ghost as well as this opera house."

"Is this place cursed because of the ghost?" Tom said.

"No. I hope not. It only seems that he's bringing people into a trance. Whenever they see a poster, a banner, or even when they wear those masks. It's like they have no control over themselves."

"You want us to look into that mystery."

"If you can. I don't want a bunch of zombies entering this opera house."

"Believe me when I say, you haven't seen what a zombie exactly is."

Raoul smirked and extended his hand toward Kane.

"Just please help the City of Paris out on this one."

Kane shook Raoul's hand and nodded.

"We'll do what we can about the trance state while we search for the Opera-Ghost."

Kane and Tom leave the office as Raoul sits behind the desk, rubbing his hands together as he looked outside the window, seeing many citizens wearing the ghost mask and staring at banners and posters.

"Please help us."

Kane and Tom walk around the downtown area of Paris. They examine the streets and the people. Kane also studies the banners and posters. He stares at the Opera-Ghost on the posters. Scratching his chin, Kane turned to Tom, who was glancing around at the Paris citizens.

"Tom, come over here and look at this."

"What have you found this time?"

Kane pointed toward the Opera-Ghost's face on the poster. Pointing toward the eyes.

"Do you see what I'm seeing?"

Tom squints his eyes and shook his head.

"I'm not seeing anything, Gabriel Kane. What are you talking about exactly?"

"These posters and banners. They're all laced with something."

Kane reached up and snatched the poster off the brick wall and onto the ground. Citizens looked on and stared at Kane and Tom. Tom looked back toward them and held his hands up.

"There's nothing to see here ladies and gentlemen. So please continue on with your sight-seeing."

"He ripped down the Opera-Ghost's poster!" A gentleman said.

"He tore it off the wall like it was hardly anything!" A lady said.

Tom backed up near Kane as the citizens slowly approached the two of them.

"Gabriel, The citizens are approaching us and they're not looking so nice."

Kane turned around, facing the crowd. He raised up his pistols toward them. The crowd stopped moving and slowly took steps back from Kane and Tom.

"If any of you want to live after this day, I suggest you back away and return to your previous occupations. Do it now I say."

The crowd raised up their hands and turned away, returning to their sight-seeing and other activities. Kane placed the pistols back into his pouches. Tom looked at him with a worried eye.

"Were you really going to shoot them if they stepped closer?"

"Would've shot at their arms and legs. Nothing more."

Kane returns to looking at the poster and grabs Tom.

"The eyes. Do you see the glow coming from them?"

Tom looked and noticed a glare coming from the Opera-Ghost's eyes. He looked at Kane and took another glance at the poster.

"What is that supposed to be exactly. Is that what's causing the trace state in these people?"

"Its magic. Someone is using magic to bring people here to see the Opera-Ghost. Once the trance is in place, the people will never leave Paris under their own power."

Kane takes out a match and burned the poster in front of the citizens. Many of them ran off from the area as Kane and Tom watched the poster burn.

"So, what's next on our agenda?"

"We'll return to the opera house tonight and find the Opera-Ghost ourselves. Once we achieve that goal, we'll end all of this."


A full moon shines bright over Paris as Kane and Tom travel toward the opera house for the investigation. Upon arriving at the house, Raoul stood outside by the front entrance as Kane and Tom approached him.

"I see the two of you are for this."

"Its why we're here."

Raoul opened the front doors and allowed Kane and Tom to enter. Raoul turned toward Kane, calling him out. Kane turned, facing Raoul.

"I wish you two the very best of luck on this."

"You won't have to worry."

Raoul leaves the opera house and only Kane and Tom are inside the house.

They walk through the house, completely silent to where they can only here their own footsteps while walking or even hearing their own heart beats while standing still. Tom carried a lamp while Kane had a pistol in hand.

"So, what area shall we search first, Gabriel?"

"I believe its best that we search the auditorium. It is where the Opera-Ghost does his work."

Once they reached the auditorium, Kane begins to feel uneasy as they enter. Tom looked around and feels as if something flew past him to where he couldn't see it.

"Something just went by, Gabriel. I don't know what it was."

"I'm having an uneasy feeling standing in here."

Kane stared at the stage and clenching his pistol. Tom looked around with the lamp. A black cloth passed by Tom, knocking the fire out of the lamp out. Tom screamed as Kane stood quiet, facing the stage.

"It just knocked the lamp out."

"It's him."

"What do you mean its him?"

"Up on the stage!"

Kane moved as he grabbed Tom from the chandelier, which fell over their heads. Slamming on the floor where they were standing. Tom looked back at the chandelier and turned to the stage, where he sees Kane aiming his pistol toward the Opera-Ghost.

"He's here, Tom. The Ghost is in our sights."

The Opera-Ghost stood still as it stared into the eyes of Kane. He pointed toward him as Kane took a shot. The Ghost jumped out of the bullet's frame and lunged over to Kane, punching him across the auditorium. Kane falls against the wall as he stared at the Ghost, which slowly approached him with no sound coming from him.

The Opera-Ghost approached Kane slowly as Tom looked around the auditorium for anything to use as a weapon. Kane got to his feet as the Ghost inched closer toward him.

"You've caused enough trouble here. Using magic to bring innocent people into your opera house to watch you perform mysticism."

"They come because they have nowhere else to go to achieve greatness or to feel greatness within them. I give them the illusion of greatness and they love it most."

"Not by my sights do they love it. They can't even leave Paris under their own willpower."

"Who would want to leave this beautiful city. There's not other place on Earth that could equal the amount of beauty and love than Paris herself. Who are you to say otherwise."

"I'm the man that come to end your reign of magic and to bring forth justice into the lands of Paris and all places throughout France. I am Gabriel Kane and I am what you fear most."

Kane lunged at the Opera-Ghost, tackling him onto the ground. Kane begins pummeling The Ghost in the face, cracking its phantom mask. The Ghost backhanded Kane and kicked him in the gun, later ramming him into the walls. Kane slides off the walls and onto the floor. The Ghost rubbed his mask, noticing the crack, his eyes begin to fill with rage as he reached over and grabbed Kane by his black leather coat and started slamming him against the wall. Tom, meanwhile, continued searching for a weapon and finds a metal rod.

"There we go."

Tom grabbed the rod and ran over toward Kane and the Ghost. Tom jumped up and hit the Ghost in his back with the rod. The Ghost stumbled before turning around, facing Tom and staring into his eyes. Tom slowly backed away with his hands in the air.

"No worries. I was just trying to help my friend out. That's all."

"You would use other means to try and fight me off. When will foreigners ever learn that Paris and this opera house are powerful in nature. They fuel me, just as I fuel the citizens."

Kane looked up at the Ghost, through his blurry vision, seeing him reaching for Tom. Kane gets up and rams into the Ghost's back and reached out toward the Ghost's face and snatched off the mask. The Ghost backed up, covering his face. He mumbled to himself as Kane and Tom watched. The Ghost stopped moving and removed his hands from his face. Holding his head down, he slowly raised it up, revealing his disfigured face.

"Oh, dear lord." Tom said.

The Ghost yelled in fury as he ran and shoved Kane into Tom, knocking them back on the floor and he began to choke them both.

"It's always those who do not fully understand. Leave me be at this moment or else suffer your sudden death."

The Ghost released his hands from Kane and Tom's throats. Tom backed away as Kane stood up. The Ghost raised up his cloak and disappeared through sudden smoke that appeared from his feet. As the Ghost vanished, Tom looked around the damaged auditorium.

"Where did he go, Gabriel Kane?"

"He vanished to another hiding spot."

"He might try and sneak up on us."

"He won't. We've just agreed on equal terms. We leave this place and he refuses to use magic in his performances."

The following day, Kane speaks to Raoul about the Opera-Ghost and gives him the great detail of their encounter and what took place inside the auditorium. Upon leaving Palais Garnier, Kane and Tom run into a woman, who suddenly stopped them.

"Please stop. I need to have a small word with you." the woman said.

"By all means, miss. Speak."

"You shouldn't worry about the Opera-Ghost anymore. He's in good hands and will do all that he can to bring good into this city."

"Excuse me, miss. Who are you exactly?" Tom said.

"My name is Christine Daae. I'm very close to the Opera-Ghost. As I said, you won't have to worry anymore about his activities. I'll take good care of him to make sure of it."

Kane stared at Christine and nodded toward her. She smiled and walked away. Tom looked back at her before turning to Kane.

"That was surreal. She's close with the Opera-Ghost."

"We'll leave the Phantom of the Opera alone. For now."

Kane and Tom ride off on their horses, returning to Rome where they'll speak once again with the Knights.

# HOD

## PROLOGUE - THE MURDER

The forest was cold, snowed in, and completely iced over. The atmosphere would cause a person to shiver in their footsteps to even taken the daring chance of walking through the forest covered in snow. Especially during nightfall where the forest would become silent as the outer depths of space. No sign of any animals either. Complete quietness.

Though, there was that one time during the night, when a man decided to take the daring opportunity to enter the snowy forest during a full moon. The man seemed to make an impression on his friends and possible lover. He took pleasure in taking those daring actions that many seem to do today. His dare was to enter the forest during nightfall and overcome the cold and shivering atmosphere.

Not even wearing a coat, he went out with only a short sleeve shirt and shorts. He might've had wore sandals, but we couldn't tell due to the fact that when we found him, he was halfway eaten and his feet were bare, his clothes ripped with claw marks and bite marks. His friends didn't know what to make of their friend's death and were too afraid to tell anyone of his daring feats.

We spoke to his friends concerning him and they hardly spoke a word besides the fact of him running into the forest with a smile on his face. The detectives however believed it to be a bear that attacked and killed him. But a hunter who discovered the remains believed it to be something more than a bear. Funny enough, one detective joked that it might have been an elk that killed him and used its antlers to create the claw marks.

"No elk could've done this." said the Hunter. "I can tell you exactly what killed this man. But, you'll end up locking me behind a steel door."

"Tell us what could've killed this man."

"A full moon was out on the night he entered these woods and we know the legends of this land."

"We are not buying this folklore tale of a werewolf being responsible, sir."

"Just hear me out, detectives. I know this sounds crazy, but you have to believe me and take this in."

"We prefer not to."

The detectives would laugh in the hunter's face and walk away to their vehicles, preparing to leave the forest and head back into town. The friends had already left the scene with little tears in their eyes and softness in their hearts. Without any ideas as to who or what might have killed the man in the snowy forest, the detectives were out of options. Until that Sunday, where the freezing rain had begun to come down and when he entered through the doors of the detective building that they knew something was happening in those woods.

# I - THE INVESTIGATION

After a series of days had passed away, the detectives took slight heed to the warning of the hunter concerning the possibility of a werewolf as the culprit of the forest murder. Everyone within the small town kept the information of the murder to themselves, most were afraid to speak to someone about it. The hunter stayed in his cabin outside of the small town to avoid certain mockery and scrutiny. He was already the laughingstock of the town months back dealing with his hunting of deer to the point where deer figured out the shooting grounds of the hunter, thus never making a return to the field.

The hunter sat alone in his cabin, covered in snow. Placing wood into his wood stove to heat up the cabin, he sighs while sitting down in an old beaten chair. The hunter's cabin is covered with trophies he acquired in hunting games. The cabin is even packed with stuffing of his kills, ranging from deer to bears to an mountain lion. He reached over to a table nearby and grabbed a book, began to read it until a knock comes from the door. Reluctant to answer the door, believing it to be a towns person coming over to mock him or throw snowballs at him.

"Go away." said the hunter.

They knock again with the hunter's patience being tested. He refused to stand up and answer the door. Going back to reading his book, he ignored the door and the knocking.

"I am not in the mood to be playing with snowballs. Thank you."

The knocks continue and increase. Nearly out of patience, the hunter stands up and walked to the door. He took a peep outside through the peek hole, seeing a man standing there. The hunter gently sighs before placing his hand on the doorknob. He opened the door and standing there is a man dressed in amalgam of modern and Victorian era clothing. The man is wearing a black duster coat, a gray buttoned-down shirt with black slacks, black and gray leather boots, and a black hat. The man's black and gray hair strands down to his shoulders, covering his ears. The man stands still while the hunter thinks to himself as to who the man could be.

"Hello, sir" The hunter said. "How can I possibly help you?"

"I heard about the murder in these woods. I understand that it was you whom discovered the remains of the victim."

"Yes. Yes, I did. Is there something wrong?"

"I would like to talk to you about it."

"I'm not in the mood to speak on the subject, sir. If you want more information on it, go to the detectives' office and they can give you all the information that you'll need."

The hunter proceeded to close the door, but the man placed his foot in between. Frightening the hunter immediately, he opened the door wildly.

"Sir, whatever you want, just take it."

"I don't want anything of yours. I only want to speak with you."

"About what? I told you where to go about the murder."

"I'm not here about the murder. I'm here about the werewolf."

The hunter paused and slowly took the time to regain himself back to normal, he calmed down and allowed the man to enter his cabin. The man entered and looked around the interior of the cabin, sighting the stuffed animals and trophy mounts.

"You are a hunter I can see."

"I am. Do you want anything hot to drink?"

"Do you have any coffee available?"

"I do."

"I'll take some of that. Thank you."

The hunter pours a cup of coffee for the man and brought it over to him. Giving him the coffee, he sits in his chair as the man sat in the opposite chair. The man took a sip of the coffee as he looked at the hunter.

"What can you tell me of the werewolf?"

"I didn't see the creature. I only brought it up as a possible suspect in the murder. The victim had marks on his body that were made by an animal and it couldn't have been made by a bear. The marks were too detailed."

"The bite marks and claw marks were very distinctive is what you're saying?"

"They were. I tried to tell the detectives, but they tossed the idea away. Blaming it on a bear in these woods."

The man nodded as he took another sip of the coffee.

"By the way you've spoken, you know a lot about werewolves I presume."

"I've heard about the legends. The transformation of man into beast. I've had family that have told me they've seen werewolves around this forest and in town. A legend that lives this long cannot be made of folklore tales."

"No. They cannot."

The man finished his cup of coffee and stood up, walking to the door. The hunter stood up and followed him. The man opened the door, taking his steps outside.

"Thank you for the coffee. You've shown me compassion."

"Where are you headed? If I may know."

"I'm going to speak with those detectives you've said. I want more information on the victim."

The man stepped outside of the door, walking in the snowy grounds. The hunter watched and he wanted to say something, it sat on the tip of his tongue.

"Pardon me, sir. But I would like to know your name. You didn't tell me your name."

The man turned and faced the hunter. He stared at him for quite a moment.

"Hod." The man said. "You can call me Mr. Hod."

The hunter looked on as Mr. Hod walked away from the cabin and into the forest. The hunter closed the cabin door and sat back in his chair and continued the reading the book he had placed on the table.

In the small town, the residents walked around the area, buying from local shops and selling from local shops. Many of whom only spoke about business ventures and homesteading as they refused to bring up a conversation about the murder and the mentioning of the werewolf. While the residents were doing their daily business, they spotted Mr. Hod walking into the town.

All the residents stopped what they were doing and only stared at him. Hod kept to himself, avoiding eye contact with the residents. He walked through the streets. Residents began to talk amongst themselves as to who Mr. Hod could be.

"Why's he wearing those clothes?" said a man.

"He looks dirty." a female said speaking with a friend.

"He scares me." a child said.

Mr. Hod looked around the small town and found the detectives' office and proceeded to approach it. The residents would move out of his way. Avoiding contact with him period. They continued to stare at him and make comments pertaining to the way he dressed and look as far as he appearance was concerned. Hod found himself standing in front of the detectives' office. The building was entirely made up of wood and stone. He walked up the steps of the office and entered through the door as the residents walked closer to the building.

Inside the detectives turned and stared at Hod, who stood by the door looking at them. One detective approached him, shaking his shoulders with a thrust walk, trying to intimidate Hod, but he was unshakable.

"What can we do for you sir?"

"I came here to speak on the matter of the forest murder."

"Why is that? You know the animal that did it? Or did you do it?"

The detectives laughed slightly at the detective's remark.

"I know the animal that killed the person."

The detective chuckled as he walked toward his office. Hod followed him. The detectives look on at Hod, confused about his choosing of apparel, stating it looked too ancient for their time.

"So, you found the bear that did it?"

"Wasn't a bear, detective."

"A mountain lion is what you're telling me? I thought were rid of those damn things around here."

"Neither was it a mountain lion?"

"Well, what the hell could it be?"

"The victim was killed by a werewolf."

The detective slowly turns to Hod and stared.

"You haven't been around that lone hunter, have you? Because if you have, maybe his fanatics and kookiness have rubbed off on you."

"I did speak with him and no. His fanatics have not rubbed onto me. But, they have given me insight onto this town of yours."

"Listen, sir. We aren't listening nor buying into some children's horror tales. We have our own fictitious troubles to deal with around here."

"The werewolf is no fabled tale. Of course, it has its place in ancient folklore, but those folklores are based on actual events that have taken place ages before our time."

"How would you know any of this to be true? You're part of the government's secret agency or something?"

"What I know, the government would kill, rape, and slaughter anyone to find it out for themselves."

"I'm sorry. But we're not listening to any werewolf stories here."

"I have a proposition for you, detective. You and this entire town of yours."

"Which is?"

"I will find the werewolf and I will kill the creature. After which, I will leave this town and never bother to return."

The detective looked at his colleagues, who were also silent and were unable to come up with anything to say to Hod.

"So, when you kill this werewolf you're talking about, you want some reward before you leave?"

"I want and ask for nothing in return for the werewolf's kill. As of right now, I ask to see the victim's remains."

"The remains are nothing but bone and torn muscle."

"The remains have clues that contain where the werewolf has headed and will strike next. Show me where the body is."

"The body is kept at the morgue across the street. You can go there and ask for the remains. They should let you see them."

"Thank you for the talk." Hod said as he nodded with the tip of his hat.

Hod walked to the office door and exited, leaving the entire building of detectives silent. Outside of the office, Hod walked down the steps and through the crowds of residents that surrounded him and watched him approach the morgue. Before he entered through the morgue doors, a young girl approached him. He looked down at her, noticing her smiling, but could sense her fear of him from within.

"What do you want, little girl?"

"Why are you wearing those kinds of clothes?"

"Because, the clothes present what I am and where I come from."

"So, you're old?"

"You could say that."

"How old?"

"Older than you can possibly count."

"Oh…." The little girl said.

Hod showed a faint smile before entering the morgue while the residents continue their frightening stares. Hod opened the door and entered the morgue building. He glanced around the room, searching for someone inside to speak with concerning the body of the victim. He spotted no one inside the room until he took a few steps toward a door and it opened. Out of the door walked out the morgue attendant, who was frightened for a bit at the sight and presence of Mr. Hod. Slowly shivering.

"What can I help you with, sir?"

"I'm here to see the remains of the victim that was found in the forest."

"Why would you want to see that?"

"Because my purpose here requires me to take a small study of the remains to understand what committed the murder."

"So, you work with the detectives?"

"I work alone. I am not from around here."

"But, how would you get the right to come here and solve a murder that doesn't concern you. You're not even from here and you want to solve this. Why?"

"The murderer is known throughout the lands. I came to this dead house to see the remains to uncover more of what I need. I know what killed the individual in those woods."

"We all know it was a bear that killed him."

Hod stared at the morgue attendant. Silent and showing no emotion on his face.

"A bear was not responsible for the murder."

"Then what could possibly have the strength to do such a thing?"

"It was a werewolf and apparently the people here seem to keep quiet about the lore of werewolves. As if you're all trying to hide something that cannot be hidden no longer."

"We refuse to speak of such folktales around here. We don't want to frighten the children and spread fairy tales across the town."

"By lying to yourselves, you already have."

The attendant leans her head down, facing the floor as if she's in shame of Hod's words. Hod approached her and raised up her head and stared, slightly encouraging her to spread the truth about the werewolf lore.

"Show me where the remains are, and I will be out of your sight."

The attendant nodded slowly. "This way."

Hod followed the attendant through the door and walked down a quiet and cold hallway heading toward the chamber. While walking, the attendant was hesitant to bring Hod into the chamber, fearing he could kill her and run off with the remains. Hod didn't say a word. Hod continued to follow the attendant down the hall and kept to himself.

*"I truly hope this is not some form of small-town trickery. Because if it is, not only will this attendant be shown the truth. Those standing outside these walls will surely know what is going on in their town. Whether they decide to believe it or not. She's walking quite slow, possibly in fear of me or what I could do. Makes no sense as to fear me. I am here for a purpose, not an assault."*

The attendant reached the chamber doors and opened them as a cold breeze swiftly went out through the opening. The breeze touched Hod, gently touching him on his face. The cold had no chilling effect on him as he kept to himself and walked into the chamber. He looked around and seen the amount of bodies that were laying on the tables. Many of them appeared to have animal-like marks on their bodies.

"The remains are over here, sir."

"What happened to these people?"

"I fear they suffered from the same animal that killed the man in the forest."

"How long has this been going on for?"

"Almost three months now."

"The detectives don't do anything about this. Who's in charge around here?"

"The detectives don't like it when we bring it up. They're owned by the upper-class elite. They control most of what goes on here. The finances, the news we receive, and so on."

"Where can I find your elite class?"

"I, I do not know, sir. They keep to themselves and appear as they please. We only answer to them. Most of us here don't even question them out of the fear of death."

"Seems to me that there's been enough death going on around here to worry about your own selves."

The attendant walked over to one of the walls and pulled out the table, where the remains laid. Hod walked over and looked at them. Pulling out tools like a forensic scientist. He glanced at the remains and took deep looks at the bones, the muscles, and the skin fragments that remained. The attendant stood by and watched Hod study the remains in every detail that he possibly could. Using a magnifying glass to look closer at the bite marks within the bones. Hod looked around and didn't see the skull.

"Where's the skull?"

"This is all that remained."

"They didn't find the skull?"

"It is possible it's still out in the forest. They won't go back and check. They told us this is all they needed to start their search for the killer."

Hod pushed the table back into its closing and closed the chamber door. He walked out of the room and back down the hallway. The attendant tried to keep up by following him because of him power walking.

"Wait. Where are you going?"

"I am going into the forest to find the skull. When I do, I shall return here and deliver it to you to compete the remains. Without the skull, I won't have all the information I need."

Hod walked out of the morgue with the attendant looking nervous as to what could come up between Hod and the skull. Outside, Hod noticed the number of residents that stood outside of the morgue had increased. They stood around him, making way for him to walk by. The residents stared at him as he kept to himself.

"Who do you think you are." A man said. "Why are you here trespassing our town. We don't need foreigners like you around here."

Hod stopped and turned toward the man. The residents took a few steps back to avoid being in Hod's eyesight. He kept his attention focused on the man who appeared to be a farmer as he wore a farmer's garment.

"Trespassing your town. How could I do such a thing when I am here on duty."

"We don't know who you are. Hell, we've never even seen you before. You must be some guy from the outer borders of the forest."

"I am from the outer borders and once again, I am here on a duty. Not a vacation. As I told the attendant inside the morgue, you, townspeople live in an area of lies. You all know the truth and refuse to believe it and accept it. You'll rather live in a world of make believe than live in a world where the truth reigns. The truth of the matter is that it wasn't a bear that committed those acts of slaughter in the forest. It was a werewolf and the beast is still out there."

"You can't talk to us like that! You're not even a resident of this town. You have no right to speak to us in such a manner!"

"I have spoken. When I return from the forest, if I am to see you or any of these people again. I will speak once more. Your detectives won't solve your problems for you and now I will solve this one problem as it affects more than this measly little town.”

Hod walked away, heading toward the exit of the town into the forest. The residents stood watch and looked at the farmer. The farmer looked around and glanced at his fellow towns people.

“Don’t you even dare look at me like that! I was standing up for you people and what do I get? No respect, no aid, not even another voice to stand up with mine own.”

Hod continued walking through the snow-covered ground as he entered the forest. The sounds of people form the town began to fade away as he went deeper into the forest. Hearing nothing but silence and a few specks of bird in the sky flying over the trees. He looked around in the snow, searching for the spot where the victim was killed.

*“By the look of the snow, the victim’s final place of living isn’t far from this particular spot. Its closer than it appears to be.”*

Hod walked past the pair of trees and spotted claw marks in the wood. The claw marks were dug deep into the wood. He rubbed the wood, searching for something that could be remaining inside. Hardly finding anything, he pulled out a knife from his coat and started to slice the tree in the areas of where the claw marks were stamped. Slicing and even cutting through the wood, a small object fell out of the hole and into the snow. Hod stopped what he was doing and placed the knife back into his coat. He kneeled and searched in the snow to find what had dropped from the tree. He picked up the small object and looked closer at it with his magnifying glass.

*“The object is a piece of a nail. The werewolf must’ve broken it off when it dug into the tree. Possibly at the moment of pouncing the victim. By the look of it, the beast is very strong and could’ve possibly killed the man with just the force of its lunging toward him.”*

Hod turned around and looked in front of him about a few feet away and seen dried blood in the snow. He walked over to it and rubbed the blood.

*"This is the spot of the victim's fall. Now, where is his skull?"*

Hod began digging in the snow with a pair of branches that were laying in the snow nearby a tree. He dug until he could see the dead grass underneath the snow. He continued digging in the surrounding areas and couldn't find the skull. After several minutes of digging, Hod stopped and looked around to see anything sticking up in the snow.

*"Where is it?"*

Hod started to walk and noticed something in the snow that laid in front of his left foot. He dug into the snow at the exact spot and instantly seen the eye socket of the skull. He reached down and pulled the skull up from the snow and wiped away the snow. He placed the skull into his bag and proceeded back into town.

# II - THE BLUE MOON

While the sun was preparing itself to set away from the town and night was slowly approaching, Hod entered the town with the skull in tow. The residents returned and followed him back to the morgue. He didn't look back at the residents as they slowly followed him and were almost on his back. They noticed the bag and tried to take peeks to find out what was inside. Hod grabbed the bag and held it tightly to his chest and maintained his focus.

"I ask of you all to leave the bag alone and let me be."

"We only want to know what you have inside."

"An important object in finding the werewolf."

The residents stopped walking and stood still as they watched Hod enter the doors of the morgue. The residence kept to themselves and not even one of them spoke a word as they went back to their regular business. Hod entered back into the morgue and the attendant seen him come through the door and approached him.

"I take it you've found the skull?"

"I have."

Hod placed the bag onto the table and pulled out the skull. He handed the skull carefully to the attendant who placed it next to the remaining parts of the victim's body. She scanned the remains in full, trying to sort out the possibilities of the victim's body. Mr. Hod carefully examined the body himself. From the skull to the feet.

"What do you perceive now?" The attendant said.

"I perceive a full evaluation of the victim. There could be some werewolf venom in the bones."

"We can do a search through the bone marrow."

"Let's give it a test."

Hod and the attendant did their part of the test runs. Operating as best as they could.

"I'm sure you heard about the other cases besides the one in the woods."

"What other cases?" Hod wondered.

"There was a couple that was attacked, and a pair of bankers ambushed in the streets."

"I was not aware of such events. Were these before this recent one?"

"Yes. All the bodies had similar marks to this one here. I'm not sure what kind of animal would do such a thing so discreetly. But I'm hearing a lot about werewolves. So, I'll take what I can get."

"Believe my words, werewolves exist, and they come in all shapes, sizes, and forms. Some are just wild beasts, others intelligent creatures."

Upon the work, they discovered the venom of the werewolf indeed remained inside the bone marrow. Yet, when removed, the venom glowed a bright blue. Its hue was brighter than the lights in the room. The attendant stepped back from the table as Hod kept his gaze upon it. Before quickly covering the glow with his hand.

"What was that?"

"Spirituality." Hod said. "A powerful one."

While the attendant gathered the venom, Hod glanced toward the window and saw nightfall had arrived and the moon's light glistened upon the clear barrier between Hod and the outside.

"How are we going to tell the detectives about this?"

"Tell them." Hod said, his eyes locked on the outside.

"What will you do?"

"Find the creature. Night has come and it's out there. Lurking. Waiting."

"You said the light from the venom was spiritual."

"Which means we're dealing with a spiritual werewolf."

"I don't understand. I've never heard of such a thing."

"Spiritual werewolves are rare. Very rare."

"As in treasure rare?"

"Rare as in Eden rare." Hod proclaimed. "Either the creature came through another dimension or from worship. Doesn't matter. I will find it."

Hod left from the morgue and went outside. Walking towards the woods. A loud screech echoes through the surroundings. Hod stopped in his tracks, circling the area, listening to the scream. Tracking its whereabouts and without notice, Hod ran toward the sound and found himself running deeper into the town and as he reached the source of the scream, he stopped and could only stare.

"What is this?" Hod uttered.

Standing in front of Hod was a deceased woman and on top of her, gnawing at her throat was the werewolf. Tall, grey-haired, and brute size. The werewolf stood up, facing Hod. The werewolf let out a howl and the color of the moon transformed into a blue moon. Hod looked up, seeing the change in color.

"What are you?"

The Werewolf roared at Hod. Moving his hand to the side, pulling out a revolver and firing toward the wolf, which runs from the shots. Hod went and chased the beast into the woods. Hod stopped near the entrance and mediated. Looking at his revolver, he nodded and reloaded.

*"I have to stop this."*

# III - THE LIGHT OF THE MOON

Hod entered the forest in search of the spiritual werewolf. Following its tracks in the snow at every turn, except for the moment where the tracks are nowhere to be found. Not even a scratch mark in the snow. Hod continued moving through the woods, hearing the faint sound of howling in the distance. Covered in the trees.

"I know you're here." Hod said.

From the distance, the werewolf lunged out at Hod. Its fangs sharp and pointed. The hair of the wolf glistened in the moonlight. Hod moved quickly and took a shot, missing as the werewolf returned to the trees in the distance. Hod breathed quietly while continuing to aim the gun.

"Just one time."

The werewolf lunged once more toward Hod, the gun rose up as it fires, hitting the wolf in the left shoulder. The werewolf slips in his steps and tumbles down to the snowy ground. Hod runs toward the beast, which swipes toward him with his right arm, Hod fires another shot as the wolf lets out a screeching howl. Hod sighs, lowering the gun slowly.

"That's it."

The moonlight looms over the wolf's body and from it rises a spirit. The spirit startles Hod without question, yet with curiosity in his cold eyes.

"What is this?"

The spirit flows higher into the air, passing over the trees and vanishing into the night sky. Later, Hod returns to the town to tell them of the news. The werewolf is dead, but the spirit still wanders.

"What must we do now?" A civilian asked.

"Take care of yourselves." Hod replied. "My work has just begun."

Hod left the small town of Rosebane. Returning to the lair of the *Symbolum Venatores*, the monster hunters within the shadows of the world.

*Hod will return...*

NEXT CHAPTER IN THE
SYMBOLUM VENATORES SERIES:

# SYMBOLUM VENATORES

## twilight of the gods

2021

# ABOUT THE AUTHOR

Ty'Ron W. C. Robinson II is the author of several works of fiction. Including the *Dark Titan Universe Saga* series (*Dark Titan Knights, The Resistance Protocol, Tales of the Scattered, Tales of the Numinous, Day of Octagon*), *The Haunted City Saga* series, and the *Symbolum Venatores* series.

Also of other books (*Lost in Shadows, The Book of The Elect, etc.*) and One-Shot short stories.

More information pertaining to the author and stories can be found at darktitanentertainment.com.

Twitter: @TyRonRobinsonII

Twitter: @DarkTitan_
Instagram: @darktitanentertainment
Facebook: @DarkTitanEnt
Pinterest: @darktitanentertainment
YouTube: Dark Titan Entertainment